THE DISAPPEARANCE OF
WILLIAM CROSS
& OTHER TALES OF TERROR

Published by S. L. Grybko, 2019.

THE DISAPPEARANCE OF WILLIAM CROSS & OTHER TALES OF TERROR

First edition. July 2, 2019.

Written by S. L. Grybko.

CONTENTS

NYCTOPHOBIA

1

"I see you brought payment, good, come in," said the woman, adorned in a dark blue linen hood that draped down over her shoulders.

I stepped into the ghostly woman's shop, a dark place which looked condemned from the outside. The inside was furnished and decorated with weird ornaments and bizarrely sewn rugs, with small cages in some places and religious idols in others. The place retained a pungent smell of spices and oils and had even more bizarre items scattered around that suggested black magic.

"I was told by a man from the seas beyond the mountains that I could find a remedy for my ailment here," I said to the woman in a desperate voice. "I suffer during the days and more during the nights. The darkness seems to promote an uncomfortable shift within my head, but the light of day brings some comfort."

"Ah, sit, sit," said the woman, "I have just the thing."

"And what is that?" I asked eagerly as the woman shuffled slowly around the shop sifting through books and candles and what I believed were bird skulls.

She crossed the back of the shop very slowly, running her fingers on glass jars of mysterious substances and stones, opening drawers and coughing at the dust that filled the air. "Answers," she replied.

"Answers?"

"Yes, answers."

"And how is that to help me? Not very useful, but quite vague."

"You mustn't dwell on a physical remedy."

"So, what then?"

The woman handed me a folded paper. "You will feel the world stir, and you'll know."

I took the crumpled paper from her and placed it into my pocket. *What the hell could she have meant?* I thanked the woman and left her little run down shop, not glancing back at it in hopes of never needing to return. The woman of the shop was the end of a long line of doctors and healers with everyone before failing to provide me with a remedy of any kind for my madness, so I was desperate and begrudgingly accepted what I received.

2

I awoke on a sunny morning, disturbed by what I

heard while I dreamt. I could not collect more than mere fragments of speech from my subconscious tale, unable to discern whether it was I speaking aloud or if someone else spoke the words. This is what I heard:

Under a starry night sky, I sit and think of what the vast blackness would be like if those stars did not exist to illuminate the oak trees that surround my home or pierce my blue eyes. For without the shy, white rays that are cast upon the moss ridden, vine entwined wood, I fear what lies beyond, waiting, lurking. In the absence of the moonlight, I am fearful of the darkness. It taunts during the cloud filled nights where street lamps are weak. It mocks as I walk the streets, copying every step I take under the little light. It draws nearer while the shades are closed. It will swallow the burning flame of day and will creep in and smother the fire that dances over hills and homes.

The words resonated with my emotions, feelings of fear and dread. It left me in a state of confusion, for I couldn't tell why I had dreamt this.

I could feel myself change day to day. My thoughts turned sour and black like the crushing depths of the sea while my body yearned for something, and glancing at the scribbling on the paper given to me by the woman shrouded by her curious blue hood, was the only thing that oddly seemed to ease my mind. I always kept the paper with me and once almost lost it swimming in the river near my home.

Daylight shone down on a heavy afternoon weeks after my ciphered dream, and beamed onto the streets and buildings as I walked aimlessly with my mental burden, half in tune with everything going on around me. I roamed the city streets going through various shops, looking through trinkets and different sorts of clothing. Upon leaving one shop, I looked up at the cloudless sky and saw that the moon and sun were both taunting each other between places above. I asked a gentleman if he had noticed it too and he merely replied with, "Haven't ya' read the paper?"

It was a valid question, so I went to the closest newsboy on the block and bought a paper, opening it to reveal that the movements of objects in the sky were being studied for weeks. Closer and closer the moon and sun were getting to each other. Beliefs of a cosmic appearance, a grand arrival was upon us, with people dashing in and out of shops, buying food and such items as if a cosmic fallout or reckoning was going to happen. I believed it to all be nonsense, something conjured up by an article writer looking to move the people in some way, but then again, I didn't really care.

The day wore on and with it came great headaches. I was at home by mid-day and attempted to sleep to make the pain go away, but my head hurt too much to be able to allow me to doze off. I looked at the paper which I had placed onto my nightstand and found a bit of comfort. I tossed and turned on my bed until I glanced out the window of my bedroom. I could faintly see the sky dimming although I knew it was only mid-day. Thinking that perhaps a cloud was blocking the sun, I closed my eyes to try to sleep but was still unable to. I opened them once again, looking at the window to see it had gotten darker out, much darker. The headaches pounded and my fears grew stronger for the darkness loomed and taunted me.

I got up and peered out the window to see the moon was partially covering the sun. Something in my head clicked. It was like a calling, as if something told me to go outside. I glanced at the paper which sat on my bedside table and left it to go out. I understood why it was given to me, and I realized what I had to do.

3

My home sat near the ocean on a small hill surrounded by tall grass and oak trees. Stepping down the steps from the porch I remember walking out with my eyes trained on the sky.

Without realizing I was walking, I found myself near the water. My head and thoughts still stirred and I was overcome with fear. My heart rate was elevated, I was sweating and was ever nervous and overwhelmed with many more emotions of malice and horror. I wasn't the only one at the foot of the sparkling sea for others too were near the water, looking up at the celestial objects. The sky grew darker and much quicker as the moon covered the sun more and more. The darkness was coming, and I was beginning to panic. I couldn't understand why I was so afraid of the dark. It was as if I knew it was concealing horrors.

The darkness now was heavy as the moon covered nearly the entire sun. My head pounded so severely it was almost unbearable until I began to stare. I stared at the ring that now stained the black sky. People awed at the thing but looked away from the intense light. Staring was the only thing that could ease my mental state. The piercing light brought me great relief, and I let the ring burn into my eyes as I drenched myself in the feeling of freedom. The bit of light that was etched into the sky was just enough to keep me from the blackness that consumed the lands. But it was then that I realized what I had done. Clutching to that bit of light from the ring, enduring the euphoric feelings while staying just out of reach darkness, I damned myself. Staring too long to grasp to that bit of freedom from my fears caused me to lose my ability to see. With this, I damned myself to a world of eternal darkness. Afflicted by blindness, I trapped myself in a perpetual dark cloud of despair and fear, clutching to any ounce of hope while I'm consumed by the blackness of my own mind.

OLD FRIEND

1

We were looking through rubble and sifting between fragments and large portions of a 16th-century carving, attempting to reconstruct what had been likely broken by children some time ago. It was a late summer day as the wind swept comfortably through the forest where the old church stood abandoned and partially collapsed. The sun was on its descent, and the little light that broke through the trees was diminishing, leaving my friend Walter and I in a gloomier landscape. With the change, I could see Walter was beginning to feel uneasy and weary, continually looking over his shoulders attempting to catch something that was not there. I decided to tease him by mentioning that by us searching through the rubble of a former religious institution, we were waking those asleep within the tombs below the old church floor which had collapsed.

"Not funny," he said bitterly.

"I kid you not," I said, "for if you step loud enough, those below us who are meant to sleep for millennia will awake and crawl up through the floor!"

"Enough!" demanded Walter, unimpressed by my continued mocking.   "Do people still bury their own in this area here?"

"Maybe," I replied. "When the Kemery sisters went missing a year ago, they put their gravestones here, so I suppose so, yes."

Walter was never the most adventurous type, but he agreed two days prior he would accompany me to the old church whose eerily styled pews faced its obscure and intricate sanctuary on the southern side of the building, and whose collapsed nave floor hid for centuries the resting places of many people whose names had long been forgotten. All that remains on those tombs are etched markings and crude depictions of what their names used to be.

Walter was very sour over the fact I had convinced him to venture with me to the place he swore he would never visit for his fear of the dead was strong, but his fear of unknown things was considerably greater. I reassured him that no harm would come to him except by his own lack of attention to the hazards of an unsafe structure.

Walter had a distaste for the old church since he was young. The last time he was in a church was when his father died, so it had been hard for him to visit this one, especially since this ruined structure teemed with old forgotten graves and the surrounding forest did little to muffle the bizarre noises that echoed through the nights and out of the shadows.

"Let us go down further," I told him, showing my obvious interest in the place. Walter wasn't too keen on going, but he followed near as I lifted myself down into the mausoleum that was built beneath the now collapsed floor. As we landed below, there was a crunch beneath our feet, and a pungent smell aroused our senses. The mausoleum was dark and with the light of day no longer there to light the way, I decided it would be best to use a match to illuminate the space. The match light revealed what the crunch came from, a skeleton. Bones were sprawled around the floor, piled up in corners and lay broken and gauged.

"Oh Lord," said Walter, visibly shaken by the quantity of disarrayed skeletal frames.

I reassured Walter that the bones were old and from nothing but small animals, largest possibly being a deer or something of similar size. I said to him that kids likely collected them and tossed them down to scare others, but that was all speculation. The rotting underbelly of the church opened to a vast space square in shape with crypt entrances lined two feet apart, each receding into the walls and along. The crypts, intricately designed, made wholly of stone with 6 feet tall doorways, were shut with large wooden doors on iron hinges made for no one to open or enter. All but one were in their untouched state; one crypt had its door open wide and battered, and the light from another lit match revealed a puzzling site. On a raised platform within the tomb were two coffins, assumed to be a husband and wife, but the husbands' coffin lid was open. We examined the coffin finding no resting body within it but there was a collection of jewelry inside, and the most disturbing thing I noticed were the scratch marks on the bottom side of the coffin lid.

Amid the thick dust floating around the grave, there was a lack of dust around the husbands' coffin which Walter hadn't noticed and had oddly left me in a state of paranoia. We stepped out of the crypt, and a faint, mysterious odor welcomed us. Walter and I walked around the large room until the smell got stronger which only meant that the source of it remained near.

We continued searching and a slow drip, drip, drip, could be heard breaking the silence in the overwhelming darkness that surrounded us and the radius of our little bit of light. We looked at each other curiously and followed the noise. Nearing the sounds the smell became much stronger and more terrible.

The source of the dripping wasn't far from the open crypt, and upon finding it, we were thrown into a state of bewilderment. On the floor was a pooling of blood and in it, I could see the constant splash of a drip, followed by another, and another. I began to shake with fear and adrenaline and

Walter could see it which brought him to panic. Sweat was pouring from his forehead, and I was at this point regretting bringing my friend to this haunting place.

Following the path up from the pool of dark red blood, the real source of the dripping was a terrible thing. A corpse of what I could distinguish as only being a man was pounded into the ceiling, mangled and rotting, dripping with blood and giving off the putrid smell that had been haunting our noses.

Walter swallowed hard and stepped back as if the corpse would come to life. I tried to calm him, but as he panicked, behind him, I could see a faint glow of red. It was like a swirl or small cloud whose shape had no definite form, and a figure whose shape could not be determined lay behind it moving in a questionable fashion as if moving between dimensions, unable to find a form.

"Oh, my god!" I yelled, signaling Walter to step away from where he was. He gasped as he saw the swirling void and stumbled back falling over into the pool of blood on the floor. The blood soaked into his clothes and covered his hands and backside. Walter was shaking with fear, and the swirl now was closing in on us.

"Get up! Let's go!" I screamed at Walter, grabbing him by the arm and pulling him away from the horrific thing.

"What the fuck is going on!" Walter cried as he

and I bolted to the other end of the large room. Our idea of escape was short-lived; towering flames and smoke blocked the hole which we had used to drop ourselves into the place.

"Seriously, what the fuck!" cried Walter once more, frustrated with the endless chain of bad luck.

Scanning the room for a means of escape from the swirling stalking void, I could see an archway tucked into the far corner of the room. I signaled Walter to follow me, and upon reaching it, the entrance revealed a staircase that descended lower into the terrorizing place.

"We have no choice," I told Walter whose face was white and stricken with fear. I yanked his arm, and we descended the damp stone staircase which seemed endless. Our little light revealed only a few steps downwards, but we hurried as fast as we could.

Below we found ourselves back outside in a crumbling place much like the rooms below the church. It was rich with overgrowth, and the sky above was dark and stormy. The area had a wealth of stone statues, intricately carved, weathered with calcium, and all in curious positions unlike anything seen before.

"What in the world is this place?" asked Walter.

I had no answer, so I shook my head at his question as I inspected some of the statues.

I had many thoughts and ideas about the place we found and concluded that it was all too mysterious, for what other plausible explanation could I have given. The statues looked so real, so unlike any I have ever seen, but what disturbed me most was that each statue had a face stricken with terror or despair.

Our inspection of the statues ended as we could see the menacing thing approaching us from the way we came. We hurried on until a point which we believed we lost our pursuer. Here we found ourselves in a circular area where statues of children all seemed to be positioned facing the center. Then that same horrid smell arose from between the stones in the floor, and the terrible interdimensional thing appeared before us, slowly taking the shape of a man. It succeeded in reaching its desired state and I Walter stared in disbelief.

"What do you want!" I cried at the thing, overwhelmed with fear.

To my surprise, the thing that stood in front of me, alive, replied to my question:

"To be *freed*."

I remember no more than what happened after my ears heard that dreaded response in its wet and raspy tone. Apparitions from the stone figures encircled us, bringing us to a daze and then nothing. I lost consciousness and awakened on my back in the view of the sun's rays and the chirping of birds with a warm breeze tickling my nose. My friend Walter was nowhere to be found, for I had awakened alone behind the church.

2

Upon inspection after that, lowering myself once again through the floor of that broken down Church, I found no violent flames blocking the way, or even any charred stone or debris. I searched but there was no trace of my friend. No remains of a crushed body or blood stained the floors and the archway which we entered to escape no longer existed. My desperate searching could find no lower tomb of statues and I didn't know what else to do, so I notified local authorities.

However, upon leaving the church grounds, with a final glance I noticed a figure of a man made of stone in a pose of despair, just like the others, that I hadn't seen before. I shuddered at its sight, and left that church and never looked back. I have not been there since, nor do I plan to go back. I can no longer count the sleepless nights as I see visions of that disembodied thing and that terrible statue; that awful, terrible statue, who, in its form, carries the face and name etched into stone of my friend, Walter.

THE DISAPPEARANCE OF WILLIAM CROSS

1

Belham Valley, an idol heap of crumbling brick and masonry, sitting quietly with ill legend teetering under its hostile stench and gloomy architecture. Sister town to Damara, a modernized erection of colonial craftsmanship filled with the bustling of people and roaring engines, late-night boozing and folk blues, was once a hub home to Freemasons and Inquisitors, soaked with the blood of friend and foe which made way for a modernized world and the industrial prowess of man. Ghastly legends traveled within the valley, and obscene prophecies depicting the evils of black magic did too. Believers of such things won't be spared, and those who believe pray to avoid the worst of which one could conjure in their mind.

On a gloomy night, fog filled Damara's streets and dew dripped from window panes and lamp posts. William Cross, a Professor of ancient history who was an upright intellectual, always dressed well from his leather short top boots to his finely tailored gentleman's coat and slicked back dark brown hair, trudged his way to the *Iron*

Chariot Pub where he would often meet his colleagues.

"Mister Cross," exclaimed Marcus McConnell, a colleague of Williams, who, being a short haired, wide-eyed botanist from the university, spent most of his days inside in labs testing theories on known and lesser-known plants. His laboratory, filled with test tubes and soil samples, beakers, and obscure smells, kept people away because of the nauseating effects some specimens gave off. With the occasional and dwindling visits from his wife, or from his close colleague William, Marcus was mostly to himself.

"Same jacket as the last week! Maybe time to spiff up the old wardrobe. I can still see some liquor stains as well as whatever else you've been fooling around with!"

"Why Mr. McConnell," said William, "come to drink up the rest of the barrel of ale like the last week I take it?"

"Damn you fool! With that attitude, your name will be whispered like my own around the school when I'm not to be found and don't take that as a compliment!"

"Don't you worry Sir, it would take only a drunken fool to become a gentleman like yourself, which I am not, thankfully."

"Ah, get yourself seated!"

"Gentlemen!" said Deborah Maldy, Secretary of the university who was always in a rush and enjoyed debates just as much as she enjoyed whiskey, "please take a seat, we don't have all night!"

"Right, right, pour me an ale!" said Marcus enthusiastically. "Deborah, have you got the paperwork prepared for the arrival of the imported plants? I mean not to converse about our jobs after hours but it's of the utmost importance that everything run smoothly with my research; a grant from the University will surely come if I can prove dwarfism in those plants."

"Yes, yes, it is all taken care of. Trust me for once, and must I say that your work is highly intriguing; many letters have come in from across the continent regarding results from your experiments."

"I'm sure over the coming months my work will be fruitful. I figured that because of its northern rarity, this little yellow flower was a promising candidate. It's isolated appearance here in Damara can potentially promote my experiments success and exposing it to different isolated conditions and interactions could show promising results."

"And what is your experiment supposed to prove?"

"Let's not get too eager in our quest for information now," piped William. "Enough talk of work already. Let's change this conversation slightly. Did anyone read the newspaper the other day, about the boy they found in the lake just west of the Redwoods? Such a terrible thing; I read that the boy's eyes were–".

"Enough!" said Deborah, cringing slightly to the comment. "Such a terrible thing, I don't want to hear any more about it. He was the old farmer's boy, the son of the man that lives on the far west side of the Redwoods. What a dreadful place to live; I don't see why that old wizard lives there."

"Wizard, ha!" chuckled William. "That old gravestone wouldn't know a thing of spells or witchcraft if performed on his doorstep! Nevertheless, a tragedy, poor boy. I heard Chief Brown declare that there'd be no further investigation into the matter. If I recall he said it was a lost cause, a closed case, an unfortunate drowning."

"Non-sense!" chimed Marcus half angrily. "A murder I think! Filled are the woods with foul people! Not to mention all the accounts of vile creatures that supposedly walkabout."

"Enough, enough!" cried Deborah once more, "I hate hearing of that place, and I doubt anything of a strange sort walks those woods other than degenerates and animals. If it were up to me, I'd burn it down, every, last tree and vile home within it!"

As the night grew on, chilled ale's and shots of whiskey were pounded down with confidence. At twenty minutes past ten, a shuttering breeze swooped in and filled the pub as the double iron framed doors burst open. What was a lively evening had everyone within the place setting down their glasses and glancing towards the doors where the shape of a dark figure stood erect in the doorway like a hundred-year oak in the woods. Floorboards creaking beneath, the character, hooded and drabbed with a long brown cloak, dirty and riddled with forest burs and dripping from the ends with water and muck, stood idle until the lively chatter of the pub continued and the awe of ale drinkers subsided. Watching as they stepped toward the corner of the pub to an empty wooden table, William stared intently. The figure pulled a chair and sat, discarding the hood revealing a beautiful young woman, dark hair, beady but radiant green eyes, thin rose-colored lips, a greyish complexion and a jaw with the curvature of a porcelain swan.

"Say, have any of you seen this woman before in this pub?" whispered William, "she has quite intriguing features, reminds me of someone from my past, I'm certain of it."

"I couldn't say I have," said Marcus, "although I do agree she is something, unlike anyone I've seen. She doesn't seem to be from this part of the city. Possibly a traveler from the south, unluckily finding herself in this heap of stone and muggy atmosphere for the evening."

The woman took off her coat and swung it around the backrest of her chair, revealing a dreadfully thin physique, frame skeletal in the most extreme way as if starved. She reached into her coat pocket revealing a small olive green soapstone, placing it on the table in front of her.

Comfortably at the table, the scholars and secretary took back drinks as they laughed and conversed in good nature. A shroud of intrigue fell upon William as he often looked back toward the woman whose inaction didn't suit the pleasant atmosphere, with which Marcus too seemed to notice from the constant lapses of Williams attention to himself and Deborah.

The mysterious woman sat for the entirety of the evening, not moving to purchase a drink, nor to remove the hair that hung down in front of her face, slightly obstructing the only attractive feature of her otherwise odd physique. As the evening concluded, William and his colleagues departed the pub at fifteen minutes to midnight, glancing while passing the woman on the way out of the pub.

"An odd woman at the most, presumably waiting for someone," speculated Marcus to William.

William paused for a moment and thought to himself, replying shortly after, "Yes, yes, an interesting woman, something peculiar about her."

For weeks William and Marcus would go to the pub, each night after the next seeing that same woman sitting in the same polished oak table in the corner of the place. The constant routine of the woman bothered William with some certainty, not solely because of the fact the woman was always in the same place, but because her unusual physique added to her mystery. There was an odd resemblance to something, something William felt was malicious and obscure in nature; something or someone he had seen in his past.

William enjoyed burying his nose within books. He adored the endless information given from history and research, with himself being mostly interested in fabled legends, witchcraft, and the dark arts. Born in a country with such a dark and obscure past, he felt it would be immoral not to pledge himself to learn the roots of the land he now resided.

After a few weeks, William stopped showing at the weekly outings, stopped attending his lectures, and this was a cause for alarm for Marcus.

Marcus grew weary over the fact that he had not seen William in quite some time. It wasn't normal for him to not attend his lectures at the University, and he hadn't been seen by anyone around town. Having missed yet another outing with Marcus and Deborah, Marcus went to see William at his home in Southern Damara, located on 23rd Street crossing Main Street of town.

Marcus knocked on the front door of the aging home; a ramshackle mansion covered with moss and vines until he was let in by Williams wife, Ava Cross.

"William is in the study Sir," said Ava. "He's been in there sifting through old books of his, I think. He's been rather evasive and obsessed with looking for something, but I haven't the clue what it could be. Whenever I ask he shudders me off or gives me a new task to perform. Once he had sent me to the University library to fetch him some books with the most obscure names, perhaps written in Latin or another language I could not read. I hear him pacing in the early hours and odd noises every so often like him moving tables or chairs. The only time he leaves that damned room is to eat, which is little at most. Please speak to him if you can, he has me worried."

"I shall Ava, don't you trouble yourself. He will find what he's supposedly looking for I'm sure of it, and all of this will be over. Fix us up some tea will you and bring it up to the study, I'll let you in myself."

Marcus made his way up to the second floor of the house as Ava trudged off towards the kitchen on the main floor. The house was an ancient Anglo-Saxon styled home, inside refurbished by William's family decades prior. Floorboards creaked and cracked under each step Marcus took as he admired a collection of paintings and tapestries hung on the walls of the home, making a mental note of some particularly rare pieces he had some knowledge of from conversations with William in the past. Every painting had beautiful mahogany or walnut frames of the most intricate designs, exquisitely carved and hung prominently with smaller framings complimenting the large.

Making his way down the second-floor hallway and reaching the study, Marcus knocked on the door to receive no answer. He tried the door which was unlocked. Pushing it open, he stepped before a puzzling site. Books lay everywhere, some over-turned, some stacked neatly in some places and scattered about in others. A vintage apothecary table stood grandly at the end of the room with papers and books sprawled across the top. Busts of well-known cosmologists and physicists were lined neatly on a shelf, covered in dust due to lack of maintenance. A large window overlooking the city rooftops was at the end of the room behind the table, in which McConnell could see the Damara Cathedral near the horizon against the setting sun, but William couldn't be found. Then Marcus heard shuffling, from what seemed to come from the room to his right. As he stepped toward the wall to investigate the noise, he pressed his ear gently on the wall to listen. Suddenly, a bookshelf beside him creaked open, startling him.

"Marcus!" exclaimed William, stepping from behind the bookcase with a lively grin on his face, "what a pleasant surprise! Please come. Come! Come with me you will never guess the discovery I have made. I apologize for not getting back to you over the last few weeks; I have been utterly preoccupied. Would you like some tea? I can have Ava bring it up."

"Already on its way William."

"Splendid! Remember the woman, from the pub? I know where I have seen her! I've been in my room for weeks looking through old books and manuscripts, photos and paintings, looking for something that seemed burnt into the back of my mind. I felt a longing or a disturbance of some sort which caused me to be stuffed up in this old home of mine for days on end; not eating and rarely sleeping. I was thrilled to discover what has long been itching my brain. Lord, what a surprise though for you to be here, all the much too convenient for I had just made my discovery last evening. Baffling it was, but very intriguing at the same time. Please come, follow me Marcus through here."

"Will, what's going on?" asked Marcus in a concerned voice. "Everyone's worried about you; what is it you wish to show me . . ."

"It is fascinating! The woman, I knew I had seen her kind before. A glorious discovery! Come, come!"

William and Marcus made their way through the corridor hidden behind the bookshelf. A secret passage laid just behind the walls of the study, presumably installed by Williams family years ago to stow away various valuables or collectibles during the Black Days. Only a few steps ahead, the corridor made its way down and to the right, getting cooler. A few steps further Marcus found himself in a room filled with what could have been thousands of books; volume after volume, much like the first room but more organized, all neatly arranged on shelves consuming every inch of wall space there could have been. Cast iron candle sconces hung on the walls, flames illuminating the room with a dim orange glow. Cobwebs filled the upper corners of the room, and rats had eaten holes through the floorboards.

"Come! Come, over here, you must look."

On a small table, Marcus could see a thick book laid on top. The book's pages were aged and stained, with a spine broken in and barely holding the pages together, with a leather cover imprinted with strange round markings.

"This is where it is, and this is where I knew it had to be. I spent years collecting these volumes, studying every page throughout my intellectual career attempting to learn everything I could. When we were at the pub, and that woman walked in, something of her physique plucked a memory tucked away deep in my mind."

As the pages turned, Marcus could see many inscriptions and sketches, multiple shapes and figures and scribbles poorly written on the edges of some pages near pictures of curious herbs and flowers and other obscure things. William reached a page in the book. Looking at the open page,

Marcus could see a colored sketch on one of the pages, an illustration of a group of beings, seemingly human but with a longer, extruded jaws, longer fingers, grey skin like the mist of a chilly early morning, dreadfully thin physiques, skeletal frames, and green eyes.

"This is her kind, Marcus! She is of another time, where Man did not roam the lands the way it does today. She must be of this ancient bloodline. She is of the *Kalterii*."

"This is absurd William! How could . . ."

"She is proof, Marcus. Look at the resemblance; it's strange but similar! The book tells of a time long ago when humanoid beings roamed the earth known as the *Haro-gal* – celestial creatures that had extensive knowledge and powers unknown to this day. They conjured up some black magic to breed early Man with spirits of another world. These breeding ceremonies created the Kalterii, creatures that rose from the pools of pure evil, grey fleshed and skeletal, dark and pernicious in nature. They were said to have been abolished and murdered by later Man for performing unspeakable horrors, lost and forgotten through the ages. I have only seen reference to the Kalterii in one or two of the many volumes in my possession. This vast collection has made accounts of many things that modern Man has yet to learn of; things that should not be shared with unwilling eyes, heard by un-wanting ears or felt by unwilling hands."

"I had pledged long ago to uncover any shred of the Kalterii through my lifetime, a pledge that has been passed down from generations in my family. I thought my venture would surely come to an end leaving my life fruitless. Years passed, drowning me in old age until by mere chance that woman walked into the pub, relighting a flame reduced to embers. A glimmer of hope filled my soul, and I dedicated the last few weeks to pick up where I had left off, to assure that what I saw was the true thing. The Kalterii live, and I intend to find them."

By this time, Marcus was overwhelmed with everything he had heard. Fabled and lost legends seeming to be real. He stood in the center of the room in a daze, staring intensely at William as he walked around rummaging through various items of his. The two walked out of the hidden room back into the main study of the house where the moonlight now gleamed in through the window.

William looked at Marcus with a determined glare.

"I need to follow her. I need to see where she goes; it's imperative I find out if there are more of her kind and where they are."

Marcus stared for a few seconds at the looks that accompanied William's desperate pleas.

"Assist me, please, aid me on this venture! Have you still been going to the Pub?"

"Yes, William, each week hoping you would show."

"Good, good. Has the woman been there since the first sight?"

"Actually, yes."

"Fascinating. Is that a yes, you'll help?"

Marcus hesitated, but it only took a chary sigh that William took as a sigh of agreement.

"Great! That settles it then, we shall rest up, and two nights forth I hope to see that *thing* at the Pub. I will meet you there as per usual hour. Fair-well."

2

That night and the following, Marcus could not sleep. His mind wavered and reeled on the brink of thought, caught in a rift between reality and myth, confused over the events with William that took place a couple of nights before. *Kalterii*, *Haro-gal*, skeletal people conjured up by black magic. Marcus attempted to dedicate some time to his studies but didn't manage to get much accomplished; he thought too much of the image in the book and could only think of the woman from the pub . . . now he felt as obsessed as his colleague.

As night fell on the long-awaited day, Marcus dressed in his usual evening attire; a brown garb with a shirt buttoned up to the neck, watch in his right pocket, a fancy pair of pants and leather shoes shined like a mirror.

He left his home, walking down the dew-covered cobblestone streets. It was evening and slightly frigid outside; a cold wind slipped and cut through the streets of the town beneath a waning moon, fluttering street lamp flames and carrying the sounds of crows and street cats. Marcus arrived at the Iron Chariot Pub to see William already standing outside beside the pubs iron framed doors, dressed as well as the last time the two shared pints of ale and whiskey and spoke with their colleague. They made their way in, the pub bustling with drunkards and women cavorting about. The men took a seat at their usual table, facing the door to keep good view for when and if the woman would show, but not in a position that bore a scent of conspicuousness. The men conversed amongst each other until William spotted the woman entering the pub, dressed in the same long brown dirty cloak, soaked to suggest she had been walking through some body of water. She proceeded to sit at the same table and pulled out the same curious green stone, placing it in front of her. The men watched her sitting idle, once again not ordering a drink nor meal, nor lighting a cigarette as most people did. She sat for

37 minutes, timed by William, until she got up from her table, taking the green soapstone and exiting the pub through its fabled doors.

"We must follow her," said William excitedly, "we will follow twenty or so yards behind."

The two men followed the woman as she made her way out and down the street. The air was much colder now, and clouds covered the moon, leaving only the street lamps to dimly light the eerie streets.

The pub was located on Bergen Street which turned into Church Street near the east end of town. Beyond that was Belham Valley, joined to Damara by a crumbling stone bridge whose rushing river water below which ran between the foothills around the town and toward the Redwoods has eaten away the foundations to a frightening extent. The woman crossed the bridge into Belham, following what was Crane Street within the town. Belham was old, small, wretched, and prehistoric compared to Damara, with a diminishing, deranged and secretive populous and crumbling facade. Its foul odor and ramshackle architecture kept most travelers away.

Lunatics and drunkards often navigated the town's streets; rumors of witches and cultists were said to dwell within the crumbling, presumably abandoned homes, performing blood magic and sacrificial rites. Putrefying houses, bow windows, and awnings painted the northward scenery, eerie laughter and moaning filled alleys and rats scurried through the shadows. Belham Valley bordered the Redwoods, a forest known to be traversed by beggars and thieves and ancient cult worshippers, which in turn surrounded the Black Lake and stretched north towards the mountains.

The men stuck to the shadows as they trailed the woman, attempting to not be seen nor heard. They followed the woman for nearly an hour until she entered by a small dirt and stone path overgrown with bushes and thorns leading into the Redwoods. The men followed closely behind to ensure they did not lose sight of her. Here they followed her for what seemed like hours, winding and climbing through small valleys and gully's, crossing streams and the occasional foxhole until the woman entered a much denser thicket of plants, managing to break sight. They squeezed their way through the copse of plants and trees to find themselves in a small opening in the woods. The moonlight shone through the leaves of the trees, illuminating the flowers below. Something seemed familiar to Marcus. He walked the opening through the tall grass, to find a patch of flowers he knew all too well. As his direction of focus scoured a small rising hill, that familiar yellow flower became more and more abundant amongst the tall grass, trees and the occasional cluster of fireflies.

William knelt and looked at the flower. "How

could this be?" he said aloud in confusion. "This plant is too rare to be this far north; the climate doesn't promote it, nor does the soil by the looks of it."

Marcus approached Williams side gazing at the same flowers as William.

"Fascinating! I just had a shipment of these flowers put in to be studied! How odd, they shouldn't be growing here . . ."

William stood up slowly and exhaled. He looked around almost in wonderment, turned to William and asked him sternly, "do you know much of this flower?"

"Of course," replied Marcus confidently, "do you need to know something?"

"No, but I'm afraid you'll have to learn something."

"And what is that?" asked Marcus who's face changed from a look of confidence to curiosity.

"Do you know much of this flower aside from its biological nature? Of course, you don't. Marcus, I must share something with you now." William moved up the soft grade and gazed towards the clouds that covered the gibbous moon. "I hesitated before, weeks ago at the pub, when you first started about your experiment with this golden beauty. It would be best to show you from out of my books at home but based on our current situation that's not possible."

The air around Marcus and William began to

get even colder, with a breeze picking up some leaves and swirling them around the hills as the darkness crept in with the sudden absence of the moon's light.

"Legend; an old tale which now seems to come too close to reality. Have you ever heard the colloquial name of this wonderful flower my dear friend? Heaven's Keys? Well, an older tale once told by an old wet nurse to children was of this flower. When the younger children were in the care of the nurse, she told a tale where the golden keys to heaven's gates were dropped from the clouds, with the flowers marking the spot they landed. I ponder this tale is true but only half true. You see, one could believe in divine beings like The Virgin Mary, or one could be a skeptic or atheist, but I fear this flower in all its beauty drapes over a more sinister truth. I fear those keys which were told as a tale, were real and lost on the earth; lost until uncovered, by the Kalterii, earth dwellers from long before the common age. But what use did the Kalterii have for these keys you might ask? This is where I am unsure, and one could only speculate conclusions. But one belief made the hairs on my neck stand and my entire body quiver. At a time, 'heaven' was meant to represent what was unknown above us - the cosmos. So, these supposed keys must have been keys to the cosmos, the space between space, gateways to different dimensions or outer worlds.

Though there was no direct connection between these earth dwellers and the keys, that book made mention of a gateway in which the Kalterii were claimed to have found, or created, or used, I'm unsure, the translation was odd."

After hearing this, Marcus was visibly frightened. Sweat ran down his temple, he trembled as he stood and his voice cracked and shook when he spoke.

"All nonsense. It must be coincidence Will, it's so ridiculous!"

"Maybe not Marcus, maybe not."

The men continued through the dazzling flowers up and down small hills attempting to pick up the woman's trail. A crackling was heard in the bushes twenty yards away, so they went on to investigate. Nearing the sounds, they spotted the woman, clearing away brush from a deeply tangled thicket of bushes and trees, revealing an opening in the stony hillside. She entered it slowly, and William made his way to the entrance a few moments after.

"You're not going to follow her in there, are you? Are you fucking mad?" asked Marcus as he quaked in his boots.

"Well, how do you suppose I learn anything by just standing about? I've come this far, and I shall go further! Stay here if you must, but I'm going."

William entered the small opening. Waiting a few moments, he called back to Marcus, "come here Marcus, come! You must see this!"

Marcus took a deep breath and collected whatever nerves he had left. He summoned his courage and stepped forward, removing some of the overhanging brush and entered the opening. It was too dark for him to see even a yard ahead of him, managing to trip on some loose rocks on the ground as he stepped slowly.

"Come, Marcus! Follow my voice! It is extraordinary!"

Marcus stepped forward a little more, bumping his head against a low hanging rock. Faintly in the distance, he could see a slight green glow.

Coming up to a turn, the light now got brighter. Through the corner, Marcus was in disbelief. A fantastic armada of glowing green stones was everywhere he could turn his head; up, down, left and right, imbued into almost every inch of the now widened cavern. "This is incredible," whispered Marcus to himself, almost forgetting he and William were still in pursuit of the woman. "What do you think it is?"

"I'm not sure" answered William, "I had hope that maybe you would know. Maybe some sort of rock that you may have come across in your studies."

"No, I've never seen anything so beautiful. It's like it's from another world!"

"Sure does, eh?" said William. "Onward, I think the woman went through here."

William pointed to another opening in the cavern, overgrown with weeds and tangles of vines. The two men spent a moment or two more gazing upon the rocks as they walked through the cavern towards the opening. William squeezed through first, fighting his away against the plants which now seemed to resist his onward notions. They had small thorns and sharp edges with leaves that looked like a fly trap. They were slightly wet as if they were perspiring, but the cavern was cold, so William made nothing of it.

Passing through, a large thorn cut his shoulder. He could feel the blood dripping down towards his fingers, but he kept on with Marcus close behind. They continued until they reached a large stone door, slightly ajar and barely illuminated from the glowing stones. It had glyphs imprinted on it, much of it hidden behind dirt and overgrowth. They pushed the heavy door as it scraped the stone floor beneath it, revealing a large opening. Bas-reliefs filled the walls of this now square-shaped room. Marcus ran his fingers on the wall to his left, while William investigated the one to the right. The room was very dark, but candle sconces could be seen fastened to the wall. William pulled a box of matches from his pocket, striking one against the end and lighting one of the candles. He stood amazed at the erected flame, shining different shades of blue.

"Fascinating," said William staring intensely at

the flame.

At the end of the room, a large stone altar stood prominently with a bowl on the top. William's eyes were fixed on the stone table. He made his way towards it, stepping up the few steps and peered curiously. An array of curious scrolls laid on the top next to the brass bowl. The bowl, Marcus could see, had engravings all around the rim in a language he had not seen before, but much like the hieroglyphs of the Egyptians. Inside of it was a dark, putrid looking liquid that smelt like gasoline and burning tin. William ran his fingers on the edge of the bowl. Suddenly, they could hear the stone door scraping closed. It shut with a giant thud. Then, William dropped to his knees, dizzy and in a panic.

"What's the matter Will?" asked Marcus, worried.

"I'm not sure. My visions blurry and I feel weak, and my arm is in tremendous pain!"

Marcus struck a match, holding it up against William's arm. He was horrified. All of William's veins were protruding out of his arm, black like the night sky on a moonless night. His cut was enormous, spewing out black sludge. He took off his belt in a hurry to wrap it around William's shoulder. But then, out of the darkness stepped the woman. A horrid shrieking sound broke through her lips. Marcus glanced quickly around the room to see other figures stepping toward him and

William, all making the same sound.

Under the blue hue of the room, he could see they all had grey skin, extremely thin physiques and eyes that glowed. Adrenaline started to consume Marcus body. He looked at William's face only to be terrified, startling back for William's eyes were black, his jaw dropping as he screamed in agony and collapsed to the floor, his body now covered in the oozing black sludge. He tossed and turned and screamed out in pain, voice traversing different pitches. The grey things made their way closer to Marcus as his friend lay dead on the floor before him. A burst of green smoke then emitted from the corpse, flew up into the air and towards one of the figures; the woman. She stood behind the stone table with the soapstone that he had seen her with before. The mist spiraled into the stone as it was placed into the brass bowl.

"What have you done! What is this! What have you done to him!" screamed Marcus as the figures converged on his position.

Then, one of the figures grabbed him by his neck and shoulders as others kicked the back of his legs so he'd collapse to his knees. They held his head back and forced open his mouth. He wriggled and fought to break free but he couldn't. The woman made her way down the steps from the altar and poured the putrid black sludge out from the brass bowl and into his mouth, forcing him to swallow. He fought free but collapsed and rolled onto his back, chest heaving as it became difficult for him to breath. The figures surrounded him, chanting and murmuring, eyes gleaming bright green and with pure evil. Marcus passed out. To his realization, he awoke, in a place where he felt time did not exist. Everything was dark, and Marcus could not feel his body. He felt like an orb of consciousness floating about through empty space. Marcus could see in the distance, places, and cities that gleamed with the glimmer of golds and silvers and blues and reds. He could see vast mountain ranges and sparkling rivers and oceans. He was engulfed by a violet and blue fluorescent sky, floating through the Aether, feeling nothing but euphoria and wondrous elation. He glided and spiraled seeing things and places that words could not have described.

He then woke in his bed to the sounds of birds singing and whistling all too familiar tunes. His head pounded and ached as he sat up in confusion. He could smell tea that his wife was making in the kitchen on the floor below. He got out of bed and walked to the closet to put on a robe. He made his way downstairs to the kitchen and took a seat at the table. He looked at his wife with joy and told her she looked beautiful. She laughed and teased him while pouring him a cup of tea.

"Long night at the bar I presume?"

"I, I don't remember."

"I guess your colleague is very fond of you, how

nice of him to get you a gift, a few weeks early from your birthday but maybe you deserve it."

"Gift? What gift?"

"The one on your nightstand wrapped up. I guess you drank too much if you forgot about it already."

Marcus's wife laughed as she left the room. He went back upstairs after finishing his tea to see the wrapped gift on his nightstand; he stared intently for a few moments at it with a curious expression on his face. He walked up towards it and then froze. He could smell something very familiar, burning tin. He started to perspire as he moved slowly towards the package. He untied the string and took off the wrapping unveiling a small wooden box. His hands became clammy, and his eyes began to water as the vapors became very intense. Marcus undid the little metal latch on the front of the box and opened it. He was petrified and gasped, dropping the box on the floor. A small, green, glowing soapstone fell out. Encased inside of it was the head and face of William Cross.

3

With the disappearance of William Cross, much trouble was brewing for Marcus. Knowing that it was no nightmare or dream that had created an illusion of Williams passing, Marcus took a leave from teaching at the university to cope. But the break did no good for him. Chatter started to form and suspicions arose from all who had known William.

Leaving the house one day, Marcus believed spending time at the school library would help him cope, help get his mind off the terrible thoughts, but it only brought more stress and worry. Through the halls of the school and in the library, he could see and feel wandering eyes locking onto him. He could hear voices speculating over his friends' whereabouts. He felt as if everyone knew he was hiding something, and they were right. He told no one of what happened and he broke into nonsense rants when anyone confronted him about his friends' disappearance. The police questioned Marcus too but they gained nothing. Slowly, Williams disappearance became a shroud of conspiracy, fed by the ideas of speculation and uninformed minds.

Late on a Friday afternoon, Ava Cross, William's wife, ventured to Marcus's home.

"Mr. McConnell! Please, Marcus, open up!" said Ava.

"Mrs. Cross," said Marcus apprehensively, "what brings you here?"

"Mr. McConnell, have you any word from William? He hasn't been to the estate, and I think something has happened to him! Oh, please

Marcus you must help me! I'm worried as all hell! It's not like him to be out so long."

"Ava, I've heard no word from him. Maybe he went to a meeting out of town?" said Marcus nervously, hoping Ava wouldn't take notice of his lie.

"No sir, I had checked with the university, they say he had no academic plans of the kind."

"I'm sure he's fine, please head home before it gets dark. Be safe," and Marcus closed the door gently, but Ava felt Marcus was hiding something, but with no ground to interrogate him on his stoop, she left.

By now Marcus had become very anxious and was running out of lies to tell. After Ava left his place, he made his way up the wooden staircase of his home and made way down the hall passing the few paintings he had hung on the wall, some of hills and fields, others of various abstract designs and Roman gods. Reaching his bedroom, Marcus opened his desk drawer to retrieve the soapstone. He took a seat at the end of the bed and inspected the object, gazing intently at the face inside. He looked away and put the stone into his pocket. Just then Marcus had an idea. He sprung up from his bed, gathered a few items like his pocket watch, a small knife, a handkerchief, and some money, and left his house.

It was a gloomy day. A mist blanketed the city, reducing much visibility other than a few footsteps forward, few birds chirped their songs. Mrs. Konner was outside taking down clothes from the clothesline she had tied to a maple tree in the far end of her side yard to the corner of her home while Mr. Konner, a very large southern European, was chopping wood with a giant ax. He nodded as Marcus walked by and continued with his work.

Marcus went for a walk in the small forest down the road from his home in hopes to gain some peace of mind. A small stone path carved its way through the thickets of bushes and trees and wound down around and over a small stream. Marcus was very nervous about being in public with a head full of information and answers. Then it dawned on him, to investigate what he thought could be the only way to reverse the curse; the Kalterii.

That evening, Marcus travelled to William's home on 23rd Street in Southern Damara. He knocked on the door. With no response, he knocked again more firmly. No reply. He tried the door, but it was locked. Then he worked the door at the back of the house. It was unlocked. He entered Williams home, finding himself in the kitchen. Nicely stained oak cabinets filled the walls and a slightly weathered wood floor spread through the kitchen. He rushed through the home and up the stairs, passing the familiar collection of paintings hung on the walls. The inside this time felt more sinister than the last to Marcus. He shrugged it off relating it to the lack of sunlight in the home, though the darkness taunted him.

Reaching the second floor, Marcus continued down what now seemed an immensely long hallway to the study. The door was slightly ajar. He stepped to it and glanced inside to see Ava, frantically sifting through pages and books and muttering things to herself. Marcus opened the door and called out to her.

"Ava?"

"Back! Back! Oh – my word it's only you. You frightened me!"

"My apologies Ava. What are you doing?"

"Searching. I need to know what happened to William."

"What if . . ." said Marcus hesitantly. "Nothing, nevermind."

"Well, I've been looking around the office and all around the house, but the best was this. This book. I found it, under a stack of papers. It's the most fascinating yet terrible thing."

Marcus looked around the room nervously, checking to see if the bookcase still hid the entrance behind it, which it did. He felt he needed to conceal what had happened to William. He felt very uneasy with the lady's persistence. Ava continued, heaving a large book from behind her onto the study table. It had a leather cover with odd symbols on it, and a broken spine. It was the book that William had shown him in the hidden study.

"What is this?" he asked, pretending to have never seen the book before.

"I'm not too sure. It had notes written inside of it. There are horrible figures, things that look like spells, but maybe even some sort of history? It is too difficult to tell. But there was one page that stood out. At the time, I made nothing of it, but it is as of my mind couldn't stray away from it. I recall William made mention one evening, over dinner; we had green beans and a roasted a chicken, Will's favorite. He looked at me and told me of a little fairy tale, something like a children's story of some sort. He spoke of flowers and other things I don't recall much now, but when I had the book and was skimming through, I saw a photo of a flower, and I was drawn to it."

"Alright, Ava, please sit," said Marcus.

"He must've been making a scientific breakthrough of some kind. He must be on a trip!"

"Ava, sit down! He's gone. I'm sorry. I have tried . . ."

"Gone what. What do you mean, gone?"

"Listen. I was with William when he, umm, disappeared. When he was consumed by that *thing*, or whatever had happened. I still can't believe it myself."

"Disappeared where? What *thing*?"

"Nowhere, everywhere, I don't know! He's dead!"

Marcus sat back in a chair, put his hand on his temple and breathed out slowly.

"I saw something, but I'm still unsure of what happened. I left this place, but William didn't."

"What happened?"

Marcus opened the book and pointed to the sketch.

"We found one, one of them, whatever they are. Nasty people, or beings, oh whatever they are! Kalterii is what Marcus called them. This must be impossible to understand, but you have to try."

With an expression on her face that Marcus could only discern as determined, Ava stood calmly looking at Marcus and said, "tell me more."

Marcus expected a different reaction from Ava, seeing as he told her that her husband died, but that he did not get. He spent hours with Ava explaining to her the cause of William's disappearance. The news left her unsettled, but she did not weep.

"Trust me when I say this to you, he's not coming back," said Marcus. "All I have left is this stone, but trust me, it is not what you want to see."

"Give it here."

Marcus reached into his pocket and pulled out the little green soapstone which encased through extraordinary means, the head of William Cross.

"It's terrible! How? What could create such a demonic thing?" Ava leaned back in her chair and stared blankly at the ceiling above her. She then sprouted slowly from her seat and looked out the window and stared into the distance. Turning back at Marcus, she exhaled and said, "I'd like to go."

"Go where?" replied Marcus.

"To the place, where my husband died."

"I don't think that's wise, Ava."

"Please," said Ava in a more demanding voice.

"Fine," replied Marcus.

"Oh, I just remembered," said Ava as she darted out of the room and into another down the hall. She hurried back and handed Marcus an item wrapped in a dirty rag. "William meant to give this to you before. Awful thing has such a pungent smell to it, especially for being so small, I almost threw it away after William went missing because I couldn't stand it, but I believed it isn't my place to do so, so here."

Marcus reached out and took the unknown wrapped object. Ava smiled and left the room. Marcus sat down in a chair underneath a light and examined the small item that was inside the wrapping. It was a brass locket with curious engravings on it. The locket smelled odd and Marcus could not discover a way to open the thing. It had a small cryptic lock on its underside and without breaking it open and risking contaminating or losing whatever was inside of the locket, Marcus placed it in his chest pocket for safe keeping with the intention of opening it in the future.

Leaving the old 23rd Street home, the two embarked on a journey to Williams final resting place. It was night time, and birds recited poems that echoed through the street while fireflies flew furiously in circles. Starting at the Iron Chariot Pub, Marcus presented the area as the origin of the previous venture. They made their way down Bergen Street toward the valley. They crossed the crumbling bridge which now seemed much more eerie to Marcus than any other previous day or night. Onto Crane Street now they continued onward. Familiar and unfamiliar bow windows and awnings led the way, turned and wound through the town like an intricate maze. Oil lamps sat lit on some porches with others hanging from gamble roofs. Marcus walked with Ava for what felt like hours, until reaching the edge of the Redwoods.

"Are you sure you want to go? The woods aren't a place for a lady that's for sure. Darkness lies within, with more hideous things creeping about. I don't even want to be back in here."

"Yes, please, we must – I must."

Marcus struck a match and lit an oil lamp that he brought with him. He entered the woods with Ava following closely behind.

"This way," said Marcus.

Traveling in the darkness now for hours with difficulty, winding and climbing through small valleys and gully's, crossing streams and passing a familiar foxhole, wrestling through a thicket of plants and trees, Marcus and Ava found themselves in a small opening in the woods. Ava knelt and ran her fingers against yellow petals of a blooming flowers at her feet.

"It isn't too far ahead," said Marcus, "this way."

Marcus guided the lady to the opening in the stony hillside that he and William had entered only days before. Leading Ava in the direction, he noticed but kept to himself that the flowers around the cave were dying.

"I'll go first," said Marcus courageously.

"No, I want to, please."

"It could be dangerous."

"I do not care."

They entered the opening, Ava leading the way. Upon entering, Marcus hit his head on the same low stone. He continued close behind to illuminate the path until turning the corner, where he put out the lamp. The armada of glowing green stones left Ava speechless.

"Please," said Marcus, extending out his arm to guide Ava towards the end of the cavern. They continued until they reached the large stone door. It was shut, so Marcus and Ava proceeded to push it open with all their strength. The door stayed open due to its enormous weight, and the two entered the square room. Deja-Vu hit Marcus like a locomotive. He moved to light a candle against the wall to his realization that there were none there anymore.

"Odd," he said curiously and confused, "these had a wick when we were here."

"Removed maybe?"

"Possibly."

Marcus moved toward the altar and pointed to a spot on the floor.

"Here. Here is where it happened." He pulled out the stone. "Here is where this happened! Here is where I can't even explain what happened!"

Ava dropped to her knees, cradling the soapstone in her hands. Marcus stood puzzled and moved to the left wall with much curiosity. He ran his fingers against the bas-reliefs on the side of the wall.

"Ava, look."

"What is it"

"Look at the carvings. Do you see it?"

"See what."

"Look. All the images and carvings, everything from the trees and people and animals, everything, they're all facing to the right . . . why though?"

"I don't know, so what?"

Marcus moved to the other side of the room.

"Look! They all face left over here!"

He moved to the back of the room, examining the

carvings from the corner to the center behind the altar.

"Bring the stone."

Marcus took the stone and placed it in a small void near the center of the wall. To his amazement, the rock began to glow brightly with the carvings unexplainably starting to burn bright and fill with color like water running through a channel. The light travelled from the center wall out, illuminating every image which by the end, depicted a lifecycle of some ancient civilization or ritual. Then a thud occurred, and an outline formed, revealing the shape of a small door directly behind the alter where Marcus had placed the stone.

"Amazing," said Marcus, "absolutely amazing."

He took the stone from the opening and pushed the door with some difficulty and squeezed through the small opening he managed to create, Ava following close behind. The inside was very narrow. Marcus outstretched his arms touching both sides which suggested they were in a narrow corridor. They proceeded onward, using the oil lamp to light the way. Marcus was bothered by the silence. He began to feel anxious and nervous, caught in a whirl of disbelief caused by the unexplainable events. William's disappearance though terrible exposed a dark and obscure truth.

"He was always like this," said Ava, breaking an hour-long silence. "He'd always be so interested in what other people couldn't explain. He would sit for hours, reading and learning, trying to crack the mysteries of our world. Many people disliked him for it, but I always thought it was incredible. We grew up together, and have been friends, and then spouses, ever since. Last few months he seemed to be less into his work, until a few weeks ago. I couldn't say anything, because I nearly urged him to do what he did; what he loved. I wouldn't take it away from him, but now I feel guilty, but not responsible. Now a lost cause, but something I must carry."

Nothing more was said. Marcus acknowledged what Ava managed to share, but to himself he kept his comments. He thought of that disturbing book with the unknown markings on the front. He thought of the dreadful secrets that lay hidden within its binding, the disgusting things that those hundreds of pages might entail. The revelation of these forgotten beings was much to deal with, but Marcus' mind lingered in the dark clouds that this book bore, a black shroud of mystery that was waiting to be pulled open like the curtains of a grand stage.

The corridor seemed to last for ages now. The stone in Marcus's hands still glowed wondrously, illuminating the adjacent walls next to the orange of the lamp. After what was feeling like a never-ending stretch, a faint light could be seen afar. The two noticed it simultaneously and gained a sense of accomplishment seeing its light. A soft murmuring or noise of what could be rats or another unknown critter-filled the tunnel gloomily. They continued eagerly, wondering what it could be.

"He would have loved this," said Ava. "Poor Will, if only what happened to you didn't," she said in a shaky voice.

The light was now closer, and Marcus could make out a faint opening. Reaching it, they stood in amazement. A grand opening stretched for what looked like miles. The night sky could be seen, some clouds blocking the moonlight. Some trees and bushes grew around what could be seen only a little ahead. The opening they exited led to a small path which led down further into the darkness.

"We must be far beyond the Redwoods," said Marcus. "No one goes far into it, we must be miles past. Could explain the rumors that float about the residents of the outlying towns of the valley."

The two walked until they reached what looked like a small cave. On the side were pictures, carved into the stone. They looked like distorted humanoids, like the Kalterii. Making their way past the cave, they found themselves in a denser thicket of bushes and trees, plants with thorns and the infamous yellow flowers. Through the trees just a little ahead, a faint glow seemed to illuminate the greenwood. They pushed through the plants to arrive at an enormous shrine that glowed incredibly. Only then, the shadow the clouds cast upon the opening gave way to the moonlight. The entire place was blanketed with light. Marcus looked around in disbelief.

"My god! No, no, no. This doesn't feel right, we must leave, now!"

The noise heard in the tunnel earlier now became louder. As the clouds parted, more of the valley was lit up, revealing catacombs wherever the trees and bushes ceased to grow, scattered like sand on a beach with such astounding volume. From the mountainsides to only just in front of them, catacombs littered the land. The shrine then began to pulsate and began to hum. It looked like liquid water, but it was dense as stone. The soapstone in Marcus's hand started to do the same. Ava approached the shrine and gasped aloud.

"There are others! There are others!"

"What do you mean?"

"Look, look!"

Marcus looked intently at the shrine and jumped back in disbelief, dropping the soapstone he was carrying. "Faces, faces everywhere!", he cried. "Oh, my god, they're inside! Trapped!"

Just then, the hum grew louder. It was almost deafening. Marcus and Ava dropped to their knees in pain, holding their hands over their ears to try to block the sound but it was too intense. The shrine continued to pulsate incredibly. Just then, at the opening of one of the catacombs, a figure exited the darkness within. A tall, grey figure, with bright green eyes exited. Then another, and another. More and more revealed themselves from the entrances of every catacomb in the valley. The moonlight reflected off their skin, showing a horrid and terrible looking physique; the *Kalterii*, by the thousands.

Marcus and Ava, in disbelief, lay on the floor at the foot of the shrine, still in pain. One of the beings approached them. Bending down next to Marcus, one picked up the soapstone he dropped. It moved to the illuminated shrine, and placed the stone into it, the stone being consumed like pressing a rock into soft sand.

The shrine then grew brighter, and amidst the pain and flashing light, Ava could see a face all too familiar to her within the shrine, and she wept uncontrollably. The Kalterii at this moment seemed to raise their arms to the sky, and their eyes grew bright. The hum intensified, rendering Marcus and Ava almost paralyzed. Then, a blackness protruded from the shrine, surrounding Ava. She screamed in pain as it engulfed her entire body. A moment later, she was gone, unexplainably consumed. The blackness now moved toward Marcus. He stared at it, overwhelmed with fear.

Then, face to face with death, Marcus remembered he had the locket that Ava had given him as a gift from his late friend William. He reached into his jacket and pulled out the locket. The chain got caught on his jacket buttons and he dropped the locket. Hitting the ground, it bounced and landed on its back, with the locket lid springing open. Marcus picked up the small thing, looking at what he found inside. Within the little thing was a small photo of him, his wife, Ava, and William. A photo taken years ago of them shortly after a time Marcus and his wife got married. The four of them in a photograph, surrounded by yellow and white flowers, all smiling.

Marcus gripped the locket and held it close. Smiling, he stared at death, accepting that the protruding blackness would banish his soul to the cosmos.

THE OLD TOWN

1

A great deal of my life, I have devoted to the study of the cosmos. Something about the endless spaces beyond this world we humans call earth, fascinated me so. I recall a period that acted as a catalyst which struck my mind with significant effect; a time that opened my mind and thoughts toward the exploration of the universe and what lies beyond.

I was about sixteen years old when I picked up a book about the cosmos; I forget the title now, but that book essentially projected the following years of my life into an exploration of the unknown. The idea of a universe ever expanding, originating from nearly nothing is astounding. It wasn't until later that I began to contemplate the possibility of multiple universes. My studies suggested that someone's ability to do, or arguably not do something, could lead to different outcomes. It is something that everyone I would presume thinks of from time to time; should I have not eaten that last piece of pie last night? Should I have bet on the short Irishmen in yesterday's fight? Much could be argued about the matter, but that's all be left to the skeptic or the believer.

However, over the years I had gone on to allow some of my time to be an artist. The ability to create images from memory, or out of nothing, like ancient structures, from high wooden and steel draw bridges to towers and turrets of stone, colonial architecture to centuries old paintings, always left me amazed. I pondered the idea that the creation of images 'from scratch' wasn't necessarily out of nothing. I believed that these images were transcended from a different place, thoughts or memories that could have leaped through time and space or dreams, to leave a slight imprint on the mind in this universe. To other people I'm seen as a mad-man, once being visited by the local psychiatrist who tried to diagnose me insane; but I was of right mind. I felt I could think beyond what others could conjure in their thoughts, that I was special, blessed by the cosmos in some sense or other.

2

As night fell one cold evening, I sat on my front porch in my old wicker chair with a cup of my favorite tea, steeped to the perfect temperature. I looked up into the sky, and just as I did, a large flash of light illuminated the lands. A meteor is what I thought it to be. The streaks shone over the city and over the dark and gloomy forest to the east. An array of colors shone within the tail as the rock burned up in the atmosphere. I sat and finished my tea as the indescribable colors dissipated from the atmosphere. Making my way inside, I prepared my bed for the night's rest and thought to myself of where the origin of that stone could be. The universe contains mysterious wonders.

Waking the next morning to the sound of Nightingales, I made myself an egg and ate some bread with milk and the idea dawned on me to take an early start to my yearly travel north. Every year I would go north towards the mountains and travel to a lake I used to visit with my late wife. It is a beautiful place. Leaves of the trees change into brilliant reds and yellows and browns and then fall and are carried away by the cool autumn breeze. The water was always calm, and a few Loons could usually be seen and heard in the middle of the lake. A small stony shore enclosed part of the lake, and an edged grass stick-out was where my wife and I would sit and listen to the earth and watch as the clouds rolled past us with their curious shapes. It is a beautiful place.

I prepared my luggage and placed it all in the boot of my automobile. The air was warm during the morning, and the Nightingales were just finishing their morning symphonies. I locked the door to my old home, a rustic place of moderate size, one floor, situated away from other people. I lived as a recluse after the passing of my wife; my mind teetered on the brink of depression, but after years I learned to cope. Friends used to visit, but I feel I had changed too much which concluded the already dwindling visits.

There was a road I used to enjoy driving on. It led through the woods, winding through the hills and crossing rivers, passing by familiar shops and even more familiar places. I decided to take it on my trip. As I drove, the sun crossed behind the trees. It fell slowly, its rays peeking through the autumn leaves, and the light which was impeded from breaking through cast strange shadows on the roadside, forming eerie shapes and figures.

It was now night. I drove onward until stopping for a quick nap at a fueling station parking area. Morning came, and I continued my venture. The road wound through the hills, over some bridges, and through dense woods, then through open grasslands and once again through more hills. I stopped every few hours to eat, rest my mind and stopped at a small shop for a coffee. I continued, night falling once more. The air was very fresh.

I kept on through the dark, making ground eastward. At this point, I decided it was time to take a day's rest. I drove through a small, derelict town. A secluded place, desolate and eerie. It was in a densely forested area, far to the east of where I lived. It was a mere pit-stop until I would continue North. Exploring the small town, I realized that the towns' architecture had a fitting populous. People wandered the streets aimlessly, likely filled to the brim with ale for I could see people stumbling about. The air had a heavy scent of sulfur or something of the like. The roads were falling apart, most streets being dirt aside from the main road through town. I explored some more until I found a hotel near the outskirts of town. Though the place made me wary and uneasy, I had to take a day or two of rest. I parked my vehicle beside the building among another of the same make, and another car adjacent which had been stripped for parts. I locked the doors and made way to the front steps of the hotel. The building was a four-story place, crumbling from the foundations with a facade that has seen better days. Overgrown and engulfed with local shrubs and trees, the area had a mysterious feel to it. Overgrowth hung from the window ledges, and the front steps had been worn down from years of use. The steeple-like perches stood proudly as storm clouds brewed harsh rains in the distance and birds flew northward away from the storm which formed in the south. I could see a group of women gossiping over tea under the awning of a small coffee shop while a group of drunks trudged and courted aimlessly, failing to win a lady's gaze.

I entered the hotel, the inside almost more decrepit than the outside. A ramshackle wooden counter was near the back of a small lounge area, and a clerk stood proudly behind it wearing a tattered brown uniform, buttons missing from the front and stitching barely holding on near the cuffs from years of service. Brass banisters dressed a large staircase and moulding was of exquisite craftsmanship. The air was musty in the building, almost choking even though the central area was large.

"Greetings, sir," said the clerk.

He was a tall thin man, wore glasses and was balding. He had a very dull expression, but nothing that could give worry. I asked, "room for one please, nothing extravagant."

"Of course, sir, fourth floor, room number 406."

3

Every day I think back to the dig in the mountains. There was a time where I was hired by a group of men, professionals, to say the least, to assist in an excavation. I was hired because of my vast knowledge of obscure and mysterious artifacts and people. At first, I could not figure out why someone like myself was asked to attend such an expedition, but then it dawned on me that these previously named "professionals," weren't really professionals, but thieves and believers. I was sought out to assist in distinguishing alien materials from natural rock and sediment.

It was late August of 1898 when we set out by plane to go far north. There was a rumour in a small town; strange lights were said to have lit up the sky on multiple occasions; strange noises filled the forests, and the snow was melting mid-winter and winding down the hills flooding small settlements along the river. It was not the season for such things, and when I was approached and told of this, I couldn't say no to the opportunity.

I was hired by Camden Richards, a man of vast knowledge concerning the field of extraterrestrials. His study was known widely throughout the academic community, but he was no pure academic. He mingled with men of deep-seated beliefs, men whose expertise were not of an innocent kind. He acquired artifacts of uncertain origin and spoke of encounters which one would not believe. Mr. Richards hired me to aid him on this venture, said that an 'artifact' was discovered; a stone, a small fragment whose nature was the most intriguing; a little green coloured stone, which shone wildy day or night.

When I was invited to this venture north, I couldn't have been more excited. I packed any necessities and made way to the airfield where I met Mr. Richards and a crew of six Chinese men.

"Good day to fly, ain't it?" said Mr. Richards, face painted with eager contentment. "Winds aren't fightin' against us today, will make one hell of an easy trip!"

"Yes, it appears so," I replied. "I must say I'm very pleased to have been called onto this . . ."

"Yes, Yes, forget the pleasantries, we must make way, it'll be getting cold this eve,' and we mustn't waste more time."

Richards waved over one of the men to grab my things and load them into the cargo hold of the small plane we were taking. We made way down the runway after boarding and having all equipment packed: pickaxes, rope, a small generator, tents, other supplies needed for excavation and of course food for us all. The plane ascended, and we were airborne; clouds past by the windows, huge airborne mountains which I only felt teased the adventure to come.

Turbulence woke me hours later, shaking the plane violently along with all of us within it. As the shaking subsided, I looked outside and could see a fantastic landscape. Evergreens cascaded over the mountaintops and through valleys; an endless armada of green as far as the eye could see. Mountain peaks stood proudly in the distance, tips so white they blended in with the clouds. I had never traveled so far north, never being able to experience such a beautiful place. Richards slowly descended the plane so we could be closer to the mountain tops. I moved to the front of the plane and looked out into the distance. I could see a small opening in the woods, and Richards felt it be an excellent place to land our flying machine.

"Better hold on to your hats lads, she's 'bout to piss ya off and bite your ass!"

We descended rapidly, almost grazing the tops of trees as we aimed for the opening in the wood. We hit the snow hard as we landed leaving no man asleep in the back. The plane came to a stop, and we proceeded to unload our gear.

"The town is to the east, about an hour's hike. It'll be good for the legs after being cooped up for so long."

Richards directed me to accompany him as we took some small items with us to travel. We entered the tree line leaving the other men to unload the plane and set up camp. We moved through the thicket, not exchanging any words. We both knew what our job on this trip was, so the needless conversation was avoided.

The August sun shone through the evergreens. The sweet smell of pine filled the air, and I could hear birds tweeting and singing harmonies and choruses as we walked. After a while of unbroken silence and melodies, in the distance, I could see a small home, smoke expelling from the chimney.

"Is that . . ."

"Yes, that's it. A lady named Aletta is whom

we're looking for."

As we passed the home, more rickety structures began to appear, some placed behind and under the tall evergreens and some built into the small hills and stone walls along the hillside. Richards and I were approached by a man, short, who wore an incredibly crude garb of some sort. It was lined around the neck and shoulders with what I could only assume to be bear fur, while the rest looked like patches of cotton stitched together. He began to speak to Richards and me in a language I could not understand. The man pointed and mumbled and surprisingly Richards responded coherently, appearing to thank the man for the information he received. I was about to ask Richards how he knew the language, but he was quick to continue with our mission.

"Aletta is this way, beyond the ridge," he said.

We proceeded forward past a thicket of bushes, pushing away the stray twigs that hung at eye level. I could see a washing tub just ahead. Sitting beside it was a woman, an older woman whom I'd say was in her late nineties, brush in hand and scrubbing away at pelts for some appropriate use. We moved in front of her and before saying a word, the woman nodded and looked up at us. I was taken by surprise because I could tell as she looked up that she was blind. Her eyes had no color, just white like a summer night's moon. She wore a necklace of fantastically colored stones, colours that somehow touched my emotions when looked upon. She had bracelets of copper, and various other objects hung around her neck like bear claws and fish bones, but the stones were the most noticeable. At this point Richards began to murmur some more in a tongue I could not understand. Seeing that I could not aid in any verbal communication, I wandered the grounds aimlessly. In the distance, I could see a river, but not much more than that. The giant evergreens cascaded the hills and valleys ultimately camouflaging the entire landscape to a dark green against the now faint afternoon blue and purple sky. I returned after about a twenty-minute exploration to find Richards sitting alone with Aletta nowhere to be found.

"Where's Aletta?" I asked.

"Gone."

"Gone where?"

"Just . . . gone."

"I don't understand."

"There isn't much to understand. Some things we just cannot explain, and they are best to be left like that. Do you ever wonder what happened to the people of the past? The civilizations pre-existing modern man? They disappeared with no trace, never to be seen again, only unique tools or pots that survive the test of time. Sometimes we yearn for the extraordinary, but when confronted with it, we can only sit in disbelief. We remain idol, lost, trapped, unable to comprehend what we seek out. I think it'd be best to leave things. We must return back to the camp."

I found it odd that Richards came to conclusions such as this so quickly. He looked like he was struck with some sort of dreadful realizations. He looked like he had seen something, and at first, I didn't bother asking, nor did I bring it up, until the evening of a few days later. Digging by the crew commenced in different locations, and as I was there to oversee findings, I spent time exploring the grounds. On the fourth night, I ventured into an abandoned tent and was puzzled by what I had seen. There weren't many things within the tent except a tall, oval-shaped mirror whose copper frame stood out with its marvelous craftsmanship though in rough shape. The glass had black spots and was quite blurry, but I expected nothing of better condition so far North. It wasn't until I dropped my lighter did I see in the blood-soaked dirt, a necklace of coloured stone. I said nothing upon its discovery for fear of what one of the workers may have done or even Richards. I asked Richards a few years later what Aletta had said to him on the first day, but he told me he could not remember much.

"She spoke of nonsense," he said, "something about hot rocks, like embers? I'm unsure. She said rocks fell from the sky – because that can happen. A comet maybe? Likely, but it couldn't be much else. A load of nonsense I'm sure of it. Spheres she said, spheres of color or something of the sort, but we mustn't ponder the visions of a blind woman."

I kept to myself that I brought home with me that necklace I found below the mirror. I also didn't share with him that the necklace was the most marvelous discovery of those few days in that beautifully frozen wasteland. We spent weeks but nothing significant showed up, so I flew out with a small group while Richards and others stayed. People were in and out of the site, so it wasn't hard to find a new pilot and a way out. The stones on that necklace though shined greatly, a bright and unusual green, very unnatural, and entirely from another world.

4

As my ponderings of the past subsided, I was met with warm weather during the first night's stay at the hotel. I could hear crickets outside my window and a lone owl in the distance. The moon shone through the window lighting up the desk that was placed against the wall near the bedside. I sat and wrote in my journal, an old habit my wife had me start. She thought it'd be best to record my day's ventures, for maybe one day our kids could read it; now I only do it when on these longer trips of mine. Then, and now, my opinion of writing in the journal was that it was ridiculous, but I find some comfort in it. It was maybe one hour to midnight when it came; a monstrous noise cried out from the sky; it was like an artillery barrage. It crashed and crackled at first, but then it subsided. I stepped toward the window and could see in the distance now a streak of light dropping down into the deep woods. Must've been a comet crashing down.

I woke the next morning, realizing I fell asleep at the desk. I got up and made a tea for myself with the old kettle that was provided by the hotel; It was a rusty old thing, thankfully the inside wasn't in as bad shape as the outside. I finished my tea and dressed up intending to explore the town.

The air was warm around the hotel, but as quickly as my feet could take me from the front doors to the street, the air grew eerily cold. Simple thoughts flew through my head as I passed off the change. The town was nothing exemplary; Old brick buildings piled through the streets on odd angles, bargeboard with exquisite gothic carvings lined most houses and buildings while efflorescence could be seen everywhere. Windows under gablets were shattered on some homes while others had no windows at all, and the sheets could be seen swaying in and out of the windows from the gentle breeze. Old iron lamps rimmed the streets in some place, and barely an area to walk alongside the road could be found without walking on the front steps of another home. After a while a small market caught my eye so I proceeded carefully toward it, minding my pockets for anything loose that may be lifted off me by the small groups of children.

I walked past a few small stands selling worn tapestries and dirty rugs, some festering with insects and mould.

It was all very, *ancient*, in a way.

After some time, I had a feeling, like a gust of warm wind maybe that tickled the hairs on my neck and forced me to change my direction. I moved windward down an alley into a large open square. An old part of the town surrounded me, with a beautiful cathedral which stood brilliantly before me. I gazed at its magnificent architecture and stood facing a fantastic set of pointed arches and beautiful windows which only dawned over me after a short while, to be depicting some sort of Pagan-like deities.

A man came out through a large set of wooden doors, to which I squeezed through as it began to swing closed. Inside I was greeted by ample, open floor space, with nothing but a few rugs and votive stands placed here and there. A man stood in the cathedral, and he stood facing a weathered stone altar. Behind it was a collection of stones and plates, figurines and busts of various religious artifacts.

"Taken . . . It is. Oh, why have they done this to us? Help us, please, help us." Said the man moaning and sobbing.

I began to feel uneasy and felt like the walls were closing in as if some unexplainable drowsiness had set upon me. I turned away from the man and started for the exit as the man continued to moan.

"Please! Help us! We have done no harm . . . We have not betrayed you! Return . . . Please! Oh . . ."

5

Darkness was setting in as the sun disappeared behind the old buildings. The more significant part of my day was spent in the town, and still the moans ring in my ears to this day. Such sadness I felt, but why? It was night, and I was just around the corner from the hotel. A drunk stumbled his way in my direction, to which he then stopped in front of me.

"Hehe! Have you seen 'em? Heh, likely not, you're an outsider, aren't ya? Well, curse these streets!"

The man took a swig from the open bottle of whiskey he was carrying.

"Ah, the only way I know to forget! She has it

you know, the old lass. She has it, it's been missing, weeks now. All them on the other side of town, they losin' it without it! Heh, the bunch of ignorant fools! Curses. Curses. Curses . . ."

The man stumbled away, and all I could smell was the stench of alcohol and whatever else was hidden under the man's rough coat. I reached the hotel finally. Home away from home. Arriving at my room, I made a small meal for myself, just a few eggs and tea. I stayed up reading a little leather-bound book that was left in the room. It was a short novel about the stars and their formations and what they appear to be and not. Just about that time when I picked up the book, I felt a thud through the floor below me. It was very faint, but enough to arouse my attention.
I removed the rug that lay on the floor to reveal the bare oak floor. Another thud. And another. It was then I could faintly hear it. An odd tongue; a language I had only heard but once in my life. Its harsh tone seemed to echo through my room and into my mind. I went to the desk and took my glasses. Seeing as I was going to investigate the room below, I left my jacket hung on the iron coat stand by the door. I made my way down the hall with the old wooden floors creaking with every step. I passed a few dimly lit candles on sconces that barely flickered as I crawled by. I entered the staircase and made way to the floor below. I estimated the position of the room based the

location of mine a level above, room 306.

At the door, I rested my ear against it to see if I could catch any speech through the wooden door. Not a sound came. I raised my hand to knock on the door when suddenly the door cracked open.

"Please leave," said a croaking voice demandingly. "Go, don't come again."

"Excuse me I . . ."

"Please go."

"I heard . . ."

"Heh my dresser, I bumped the table, damned thing. Leave".

The door slammed in my face, and I stood in confusion. Just then I heard another coupling of noises. This drew my attention, and I could not help to be curious. I looked down toward the door lock, which had a sizeable keyhole. I bent down to peer through the keyhole and through it I could see a couple of people standing. It was very dark in the room, but the only source of light was an orange glow that cascaded the walls. Now I can't entirely recall what I heard, but this was my recollection of the conversation:

Figure 1: "Welcome back to civilization my friend. How was the trip?"
Figure 2: "Rough. Cold, heh, I still say you should have come along. I cannot begin to tell you the things we have uncovered."
Figure 1: In due time, over a tea, how about that?

But nevertheless, a discovery that'll change the world I hope; a revelation, that'll make me a rich man."

Figure 2: Why yes Mister -----, such things are possible, heh.

Figure 1: Probable . . . Likely would be better.

Figure 2: Yes, yes, of course, sir.

Figure 1: And the stones? You made mention of them.

Figure 2: Yes sir, magnificent artifacts. Such wonders those stones are. Bad things they are. Careful handling is a necessity.

Figure 1: Dangerous?

Figure 2: Very. You see, the expedition though fruitful, did come to a price. We lost many men out there, many.

Figure 1: From the snow? The cold?

Figure 2: Heh, that was the least of my worries; *the stones.* Have you ever seen a man, suffer? Have you ever seen a man, or heard a man, cry and scream horrifically, or have an insatiable thirst for blood? I have, and these men, all their voices, ring true in my ears, even now.

Figure 1: You will be compensated, well.

Figure 2: Yes, I'm sure, but I feel that that may not be enough.

I remember what I saw next through that keyhole. A bright light engulfed the room after the last man spoke, and I heard, such a horrific scream;

a scream of pure terror that I may never forget. As that light illuminated the room, I could make out two distinct things. Firstly, a collapsed body sprawled on the floor, disfigured and disproportioned. The second was the man that had previously answered the door. He stood prominently over the mangled body, heaving heavily, heavy like an exhausted beast after a vigorous kill. A glowing green item lay on the floor at his feet, casting a shadow on the wall. After a couple of moments, he turned and looked up. The man's and my eye made contact through the door, and my heart dropped into my stomach.

"You!", he snarled, pointing through the door at me.

I could see on his face the amount of anger that now consumed him. He darted towards the door, and I fell back in a scramble to get away. I headed down the hall and could hear behind me the door to the room open and heavy steps of the man following. I went up the staircase and dashed into my room and shut the door, leaning against it to hold it closed. Out in the hall, I could hear the man's footsteps, slowly weighing down on the old and creaky floorboards. I bent over and peered through the keyhole of my door in hopes to see where he was. To my horror, he was looking back at me through the keyhole, but his eyes were terribly void of color, black with hate. The man pounded violently on the door, screaming for me to open it. I could hear the rage that was engulfing him, and his voice became deeper and more animal-like. The pounding continued as I frantically looked around the room for a weapon. Nothing. The violent attack on the door then ceased, and I stood back from the door slowly, not averting my gaze. I could see through the keyhole and through the crack underneath the door that the candles in the hall had been put out. I turned my gaze toward the window and realized I could push it open and climb out. I lifted the window frame, sliding it up the track and peered out below. Down below my vehicle was luckily parked almost perfectly in line. Suddenly, the door to my room began shaking violently, and it broke open, and through the door, I could see a horrid physique standing tall in the doorway. Cold air filled the room, and I could see my breath as well as the man's breath in front of me. He rubbed his head but did not look away from me. I could almost feel him trying to enter my mind. The strangest feeling overwhelmed me, as if dark magic was surrounding me. The man began to *change*. A blackness formed around him, and in the little light that remained in the room, I could see the reflection of something silver hanging around his neck. Then, under murmurings and nasty vocal sounds, the transforming man began a sprint directly at me. I turned in horror as quick as I could and prepared to jump out the window when he pulled me back by my jacket with one hand and slammed me to the ground. As the man stood above me, I could see him holding his head in pain, and with this, I did not wait. I scrambled to my feet and went for the door, leaving the man behind me in the room, groaning and growling. I sprinted down the hall to the stairs and continued out of the old and withering hotel knowing that the deranged man was not far behind. I ran into the wooded area behind the hotel. A full moon illuminated the sky and seemed to reveal a path ahead of me as I ran in fear of death. I ran until the point exhaustion almost took over, when just beyond a dense line of trees and bushes, a small river and a few formations of stones, I could see a church. It was old and crumbling and extremely aged. Its stained-glass windows were mostly overgrown with the greenery that surrounded it and at its front side above the doorway was an overwhelmingly horrific depiction of some god. I ran up the towering stone stairway and pushed open the large wooden door that kept this dreadful looking building shut, looking for shelter. Closing the door behind me, I turned to a grisly site. Inside where an alter used to have been, was what looked like a shrine with skulls sprawled over every possible nook and cranny. Candles were placed in any gaps, inside skulls and outside and around. This church looked much like the previous with obscure deities abound. Beside the shrine a wooden table stood with piles of rope tossed over it, drenched in blood, with more pooling beneath it. The entire church had a pungent odour that stung the senses and caused the eyes to water. Here I ran behind a rack of iron forks and large brass candle stands that stood prominently next to pots of black berried shrubs that were placed in painted clay pots. Just as I had found a place to duck behind, the wooden doors burst open and in came the following man, or what was left of him.

I could see through the plants and brass pieces that the man was almost no longer a man, but a beast. A horrid looking thing he was and almost indescribable too. His head had dropped from his shoulders down to the center of his chest, and his shoulders seemed to have dropped an equal distance as well. His arms were extruded in length, and the definition of his muscles entertained the idea that intense starvation had occurred in the little time between the church and the hotel. His clothes were now stretched, tattered and missing, and he had large growths on his back and waist. This now horrid creature stood panting in the doorway of the church, looking around for its first victim of what would be a cruel and undeserving death. It crept slowly, scouring the area for me as I looked on as still as I could, doing my best to not give myself away. The beast let off a call that was horrifying to listen to. I put my hands over my ears, and in doing so, I managed to knock down one of the candles off the brass work that held it up. It dropped to the ground, and the noise drew the beast's attention my way. As it stepped nearer, the front doors now burst open, and a mob of men came in with guns and hatchets and other sharp ended weapons. Luckily, the beast turned its attention away from me and to the door, granting me the chance to escape but the door remained blocked by the mob.

"Banish this thing from our lands!" cried who I deemed to be the leader of the mob, which now looked to be a hunting party. "Spill its blood across our sacred floor and let it not be born unto us again!"

The party now attacked the beast and not long after did they have it pinned down with its legs and arms in a hold. With the loss of a few men, the remaining brought the beast to the altar. It thrashed and groaned and fought as much as it could. I dashed from my hiding spot towards the front of the church, nearing the way out. While sitting still in the shadows, I looked towards the altar with the party of men and the beast. The leader took a long blade and sliced the throat of the creature and its blood sprayed and spilled everywhere.

Taking off its head, the leader held it high and cheered, "Banish the curse, rid the unholy, kill the devoid of consciousness!"

That grueling site left me trembling and

sweating profusely. I crept toward the door, and just as I had reached it, I heard the leader cry out to me, "You! Witness! Bring yourself here so that you may share in the glory of our holiness!"

I couldn't stand the site of everything around me, so I dashed out the door as quick as I could, knocking over an array of candle sconces that crashed down behind me.

Much after that, I do not remember. I left that wretched place, cursing it as I drove away into the sunrise of the next day. Weeks later when I was in a city, I stumbled upon an article that was headlined in the newspaper.

It read:

Tuesday, August 14 of 1901

MURDERS & FIRE IN VALLEY COME TO LIGHT

Wilburton Village victim to murders. Village residents savagely killed and dismembered, prompting an investigation by local authorities. The disappearance of locals prompts questions. The local church burned down.

A few weeks later after the charred remains of the church had been excavated, a follow-up article was posted in the newspaper declaring that bodies were discovered within the burned down building. The paper, while claiming those caught within had committed suicide due to their abhorrent crimes concerning a dark following that seemed to be gaining a foothold in the northern parts, but what I knew the truth to be, was that those caught within fought valiantly against an evil creature.

6

Weeks passed until a could sit comfortably after having pushed down the realization that I started that fire, killing those people. One thing I could mend between these memorable occurrences was that the thing that was present at the deaths of Aletta, the beast-man, and the people of Wilburton Town, was that an inconspicuous green stone seemed to mysteriously be at the center of it all. This stone, steeped in mystery and shrouded with death promoted nothing but endless thoughts.

On an cool morning in September I sat on my front porch in my old wicker chair with a cup of my favorite tea, steeped to the perfect temperature. On the table lay my favorite book, and next to it burned a cigar. Glancing at the infamous fracture of green that was now nailed into the porch doorframe, I looked up into the sky. A large flash of light burst out illuminating the lands.

Happiness.

KIRIHYYL'S HORROR

1

I write this as I can only see the end is near. Whoever recovers this withering book, bound by aged red leather, will find what could seem to be a scribbled tale of my last accounts within a dreadful place, victim to a horror that would make one without strong will shudder. I have found solace in writing, but I cannot muster the strength to carry on. Even if I could, insanity would consume me.

In this book on its weathered pages, you'll find a crude recollection of my experiences and conversations as well as some final insights. The one thing I must stress is to seek no further knowledge of the matter after the discovery of these writings, for all that can be found are unspeakable horrors and the ravaging and torturous mistreatment of the soul.

Before my grim end, I embarked on what was to be a promising and fruitful journey with colleagues, scholars, and friends. Wilbur Vardé, a Frenchman I had met at a workshop through *The Company*, and Alfred Hamburg, a conspicuous gentleman, and slightly narcissistic but trusting soul were some of these colleagues mentioned above.

Alfred was of an ilk that was unlike my own. He was a criminal, a man that not many would tread with, granted this was only known by myself, and I believe a few others because he blatantly spilled this knowledge over a couple of whiskeys a few weeks back to me, so I would only presume that this has happened before. Alfred was a rugged-looking chap with dark brown hair slicked back and dirty which made him appear like he had a head coated with motor grease. Although he dressed in a tasteful fashion with linen suits and vests made of silk, I could only ponder the number of pieces that had been buried or burned due to the outcome of altercations because of his shorter-than-most temper. On the other hand, Wilbur wasn't the most sociable individual. He came up a poor lad who had a difficult life in adolescence, but at even times like these, it wasn't odd to hear of children enduring difficult times as a youth. The Great War swept through the towns and had people in a state of disarray, panic, and misfortune, but some coming up through this kind of life, like Wilbur, became slippery individuals.

A traveller from the Amalfi Coast was another one of these scholars and friends mentioned prior: Madina Faretti. Her drive for discovery and adventure was what made her an unconstrained student of the world. She was the most intelligent of us all, often rambling about the ancients and discoveries she wished she made herself. She specialized in Egyptian and South American relics and languages while possessing a variety of other impressive intellectual qualities and abilities.

We had been collected by the Company to aid in an excavation south of the Americas on an island very rarely frequented by outsiders. With a small town which was now crumbling and decrepit, the island bore a branch of people very different from the common man or woman. They had their own language which very few people knew, and their ways suggested a simple life with minimal scientific advances.

Our tour embarked on a long voyage by sea, on a small steel ship named *Grit*. Its rusted hull broke through the mighty sea waves with surprising ease. The port and starboard rails were chipping away of their grey paint while the wooden floorboards creaked and moaned after every step, some blistered and so dried out from the blazing sun that they cracked and split, injuring the occasional weary and beat down seaman. Most nights I gazed upon the stars as the boat worked through the water, fighting the rabid ocean yet gently dancing with the waves. The sky revealed every evening what seemed like tens of thousands of little lanterns, sitting indescribably far, so far one could not comprehend. Most nights during the spring, a young boy could be seen dancing in the black sky, with a steed not too far away, watching over the boy; a tale once spoken to me when I had been a young boy.

On a clear evening with a waning moon whose light reflected beautifully against the sleeping ocean while I silently spoke with the stars, Madina came to my side. She too stood in silence as we both looked ahead beyond the waves and beyond the skies. I recall this conversation with some ease for just before any words, I felt an overwhelming sense of peace.

"Beautiful, don't you agree?" said the lady of wide greenish blue eyes.

"Of course, something you can't take for granted," I replied.

"Like a treasure map with an X?"

I laughed, "Yes. Suppose we find anything?"

"It is a possibility, would be better if only I were there for the discovery, but maybe I can grow accustomed to your company."

I laughed once more because by this time I knew that Madina yearned to make a discovery of her own. It had been years since she had anything to bring to the museum which she discovered or recovered alone. Museum was not the best word to use, because she was more of a procurer for private collectors but had the occasional run-in with a legitimate institution. She was a beautiful lady of the boot, with her greenish blue eyes and dark hair. She was an experienced yet slightly rugged person, who still maintained a radiant complexion, a complexion which could send a fool to the depths of oblivion if they gazed upon her too long and fell for her charm.

2

Our trip by sea ended weeks ahead of schedule. Our captain, Francis Hale, claimed a favorable current had been our ally, bringing us to Kirihyyl's shores. We docked at the coast at a sizeable wooden dock comprised of blistering planks and rotting pieces; Kirihyyl once having a glorious fishing hamlet, now an eerie place with the stench of rotting fish that contaminated the air. Next to this horrid stench filling every breath, smoke from down the shoreline surged from the seaside fires the inhabitants lit on foggy days like this day and chilly nights when the sea breathed cold winds.

"It used to be better here," said Hale, lighting a pipe as his crew and ours unloaded equipment and materials from the ship.

"Kirihyyl used to be a wondrous place, blue skies, rich sea life, the sweet smell of fish and squid being roasted but now, it's changed . . . something's changed."

Hale's face turned sour as he looked around.

"These fuckin' people have run it down. They shouldn't be living 'ere. There was a different folk who used to reside on these beaches, but they were pushed out you hear. Savages, these people, inbreeds and broken folk, took what wasn't theirs and claimed it their own. Great business here though!"

I looked curiously around as some folk gathered close to the shore to watch as our things were unloaded from our rusty ship. The waters were black below us, suggesting the ocean floor was either far below the surface or the water was much less than ideal for swimming.

"There's a shelter for you down the beach, small houses with red roofs, and you'll stay there until your guide from the dig site comes to greet you in the morning," said Hale. "In the meantime, get comfortable, and try not to pass out from holdin' your breath for too long."

"A guide?"

"Yes sir, the site is far up into the hills in a fascinating place that I think you'll like. The locals don't wander too far from their homes on the shores, so most don't even know what's beyond the first few trees."

"Interesting place?"

"Erg, yes, heh."

"Care to venture that?" asked Alfred.

"You'll see soon enough my friends, don't you worry there isn't much to worry about up there, depends on if you believe in folk tales and such things. I'd love to tell you about such horrid things, but I got a nice bottle o' rum waiting for me in my quarters, and unfortunately, I am no storyteller. Ask around if you so wish." Hale laughed to himself and walked up the boardwalk leaving us to find our own way.

The stench of fish got worse the closer we all got to the land. Derelict homes sprawled the seaside forming narrow ways. The main dock ended at an open street, which wasn't much of a road but more a muddy opening with paths into the hills. To the east homes were erected in a seemingly random fashion with only footprints dictating where walkways were between their water-soaked walls. Water dripped from the gable roofs, and more of this sporadic settlement could be seen to the west. Lanterns hung from under the rooftops and cats could be seen jumping from home to home taking no notice of our arrival. A chilly breeze tickled the skin and kept lanterns and store signs swaying, causing a constant chilling squeak that was indeed unending.

Further up, some locals could be seen making creel's while others cooked what I could only discern to be some type of sea creature that looked native to the island's waters. Exploring the area, we made the sight of the red roof building that Cpt. Hale mentioned we would be staying in until the arrival of our guide. It was a large building comprised of two floors. A staircase spiraled from the muddy sand and stone below to guide the way up to the main floor of the building. Each stair step moaned under the weight of our bodies as we climbed up to the first floor. Two large wooden doors with iron bar windows lay open at the front and inside was a small oak desk that looked to date back to the 1700s. Gold plates with intricate works of ships and treasure covered the entirety of the desk, with rubies, sapphire, and jade being forged into the wood and metal along with phenomenal carvings of people being praised by others, some sort of religious piece I could only presume.

An old woman greeted us upon entering the room; her face was extremely wrinkled and her skin pale like the moon. Her clothes were tattered and dirty, and she wore a long brown garb with various pieces of jewelry on her wrists, fingers, and neck. She reeked of fish and tobacco and had a slight hint of alcohol still on her breath. Her hair was grey and balding in some places, and her eyes were small and beady, giving her a sharp look of suspicion. The very sight of her gave me chills but then again, I was lucky to have company of some who in theory were likely more terrible souls than this woman.

"I assume you landed with Mister Hale?" said the beady-eyed woman.

"Yes," replied Wilbur, stepping closer to the lady. "I must ask but do we have a selection to choose from for our rooms? I require a specific type of orientation when it comes to sleeping quarters."

"You'll get what we can spare, most rooms are full."

"Full? With what, people?" chuckled Madina. "It looks like there's no one in town!"

"Best you mind yourself, woman," said the lady bitterly. "We have a room for each of you, so select amongst yourselves and do what you must to get comfortable. Do not stray too far from the building at night, for the tide comes up high enough that if you wander too far, you'll be lost for good."

The old woman pointed down a hallway to the left of the wondrous desk she stood behind, and we proceeded to select rooms for the night. I did not care which I received, so I took the smallest one. A small bed was inside with nothing else but a wooden coat rack, a small side table and a desk big enough for me to write a bit into the journal that I carried with me. I unloaded some of my clothes and sat down, pulling out a small bottle of liquor I had stowed away with my personals. I poured myself a glass, took off my shoes, drank and dreamt of the day to come.

3

The next morning, I woke to the sound of

shrieking crows that resided within the treeline not too far behind the building which we slept. I didn't sleep well, for nightmares poisoned my dreams with visions of phantoms and night dwellers that crept silently. This hadn't been the first time I had these dreams. In anticipation of this journey and before casting off from home on that rusty heap of steel, night dwellers haunted me. Something called to me in my dreams, almost speaking to me, whispering strange words and sounds. What I could only interpret as the peak of my lucid trance, through a fog of haze and memory loss were the words or even feelings that communicated a name: *Umal*. I could not make sense of what this was, for everything was a blur and that phrase being the only remnant of my slumber.

At the sound of knocking on my door, my attention turned from my thoughts to reality.

"Let's go, Gael. Gather your things, we leave shortly!" said Alfred, eager as a barnyard rooster at dawn.

I gathered some of my items: my journal, a water canteen, some small packets of food rations along with matches, a pocket watch given to me by my grandfather, and a pipe with a small tin of tobacco. I dressed in my usual attire, boots, and dark brown trousers, a maroon leather jacket and a wool shirt underneath. I slicked back my blonde hair and put a hat over my head.

Making my way outside of the hotel, passing

the large oak desk that I admired so much, I rallied with Madina, Alfred, and Wilbur, who were all eager and waiting on my tardy appearance.

"'Bout time. We have a short walk into the trees, and we'll meet our guide there" said Alfred, picking up some of his things while the rest of the men loaded items into a horse's wagon.

We stumbled onward up the path making no conversation, for the place we now journeyed through seemed to gradually bare a stranger and gloomier appearance. Buildings appeared to be abandoned, once built by wicked people, doing what I could only imagine were more evil things behind closed doors. The crows seemed to never let up; their chirps and what seemed like constant teasing drove us insane . . . or at least drove me insane.

Tall grasses combed over the stones and grew from between, and the old trees that swayed in the chilly wind moaned and fluttered and cracked, causing worry of imminent death by a falling giant. After walking where we were told to go the first day, the hills began to get steeper and what seemed like a trench began to form between the hills and mountains that led further into the land. From just beyond, a crackling of branches and bushes could be heard, as if an animal the size of a bore was making its way towards us. The unknown beast appeared to be getting closer, causing wariness among the party. Just then a man with a long white beard appeared from the overgrowth. He wore workman's boots and a leather belt, strapped with various digging tools. He wore a frayed brown hat with a small gold emblem on its side, and a long-sleeved shirt dirty and doused with sweat. He stepped out in front of us almost panting but realizing he reached us, a broad smile spread across his face.

"Well then! You must all be the discovery team! Err, or the diggers, erg, or professors! None the less, let's get a move on, it'll take time for us to get where we're going and night falls fast on these lands!"

"Sir," I said with uncertainty. "Are you the guide? What were you doing in the treeline?"

"Oh, oh, just took a detour you see, old soul like myself, little adventure comes here and there, thought it best to keep me on my toes!"

"Isn't the excavation going to be some adventure?" chimed in Madina.

"Right, oh yes, but seeing as I'm not one doing much physical work, it's best I get my legs movin' when I can, ha!"

The gentleman's cheerful attitude seemed to calm everyone down and gave us a little bit of hope in this dark place.

"We'll have to travel up to the dig site through the woods, it'll be a long walk especially with all this equipment of yours, but a little proactive thought should keep you busy. Oh! My manners, living out here makes me forget about some of the things from back home. It's been a long while . . . My name is Silas, Silas El Morani."

"A pleasure to meet you," said Alfred, reaching for Silas' hand but Silas turned away abruptly as if not noticing the outstretched.

After the brief and awkward encounter with Silas, the men gathered the equipment and carried on up the way between the cascading mountains.

The air became thinner, the fog denser, the crows louder and the wind colder. Not much of a holiday but a promise of potential wealth paved the way for the four of us who were here for academic or personal purposes. Now, Madina seemed to feel weary and tired. Perhaps the extended duration of walking began to take a toll on her, but the rest of us seemed to have no problems. The walk was grueling and seemed unending. The beauty of the land was more prominent the higher up and farther we got into the mountains, but there remained a sinister feel which I could not explain. The treetops down below seemed to almost dance with the winds coming from the ocean and through the wicked dilapidated town. The various paths and creeks formed almost words in the landscape below, like a message to the gods above. Near this point in our journey, I inquired to Silas about the discovery of the site.

"In August of 1894, a young boy left the

Kirihyyl shore under a waning moon, disappearing into the treeline with his mother crying out from her home" said Silas. "The boy ventured up into the hills like us now, scrambled through the thick brush and the winding brooks. After hours of running, he stumbled upon a clearing to find a graveyard deep in the trees. Hundred-year-old oaks surrounded the place, and monoliths stood greatly as if touching the black and blue sky. The graves he had uncovered seem to bear names, but of another language that he could not read nor understand. While exploring the area, he walked down a small depression and the soil gave way sending the boy into a cavity within the hills. He tumbled down a distance into the darkness, but there appeared to be a faint light some way forward. The boy proceeded for that was his only option; climbing up from which he fell was almost impossible for the jagged rocks, being a miracle he didn't die on the way down. Onward he went and found a cavern with light pouring in from above. This place appeared to be a hub with a system of passages that led in all directions. Through a miracle, he chose a tunnel which after hours of walking, brought him to the shore on the other side of the island. Upon his return, beat up and scratched, soaked and riddled with dirt from his feet to his head, the boy told his story to the town warden. He brought the warden to the place which he came from, only to find that the tide had risen so high that the opening of the tunnel was lost to the sea, and the water never receded."

"Seems that there was nothing there to be found, no? Just a system of tunnels?" I asked.

"Yes, but what the boy later disclosed in 1898 at the age of fourteen years to one of the priests in confidence through confession, was that he was called to the trees by a voice in his head, and that a figure led him through the woods, a figure whose appearance he would not describe for fear it would poison his thoughts. The hub that he also seemed to reach had a stone altar or monolith carved with intricate depictions of death and life, fortunes and relics of a past world."

"Ah, so that is what the search is for, the altar."

"Or the relics" chimed in Wilbur, feverish with intrigue.

"And why did the Priest share this information when it was entrusted to him in the name of God?"

"Arthur Murin was a man of faith. He was from south England and was trusted by the less than respectable locals from the more wicked parts of the country. But with an ear as large as Gods, hearing all from the filthy and stained souls, Arthur acquired secrets that the common man wouldn't know. With his knowledge, he realized that it was unsafe to stay and that his safety was in jeopardy from an enemy he could not name nor describe. Arthur left England and came to

Kirihyyl, trusted by the deprived and wicked people to their secrets. He now sits in the church further up in the graveyard the boy discovered that August night in a constant state of prayer. He sees things in the darkness, and claims that a shadow blankets his soul bringing him further and further from sanity."

With this information, my mind tended to wander more often than before.

We had settled down in the mountains in a small clearing and pitched tents, put out cots and small tables for meals. Most of the men sat and drank as night fell and a full moon's light bathed the treetops and surrounding formations of rock and waterways. Alfred and I pitched a tent which the two of us took as a refuge from the insects flying and crawling about.

Madina and Wilbur had their own tents set up, much smaller than ours, and further away from the rest of the party, likely to keep away from the boozed men laughing and singing folk songs from home. Beside our cots was a small wooden table which I used to place most of the belongings I kept with me: a small watch, a knife with a beautiful steel blade, and cigarettes. I also carried with me a handkerchief made of silk, given to me by my late mother as a gift, passed down from generations. Alfred placed upon the table a pocket watch of his, a delicate gold piece with a ruby as the crown, a small tobacco pipe with its accompanying tin, and to my astonishment, a revolver, fully loaded with 6 rounds.

"What's the need for that?" I asked Alfred as I stared at the weapon.

"Weird thing to bring, you think? So be it then. Need? No need. A precaution I suppose. Never know what'll be about in a place like this. Best to keep some guard up! Ha! Don't you worry, I never had to use it before, don't plan on using it 'ere."

"Do the others know?"

"They'll be damned if they didn't think the same!"

Alfred proceeded to pick up the revolver and examine it.

"I'd think that you'd come prepared. A place like this, shrouded by night. He who'd find the key to the lock that guards the palace, best have a lock to his soul and pray that the key not be discovered."

I didn't know what he meant by this riddle, but I believed Alfred was hiding something, but I was in no place to question him.

A terrible storm came that night while we slept on our rickety cots that were set up as best as they could be on the uneven Kirihyyl mountain grounds. The winds wailed and beat down our tents and threw smaller items that weren't tied down. The lamp that hung from the center of mine and Alfred's tent squeaked as it swayed back and forth, keeping me from slumber. The noises coming from beyond the canvas of our tent were loud and distorted; trees were cracking, bushes were rustling – I could even hear sounds of a boar or some creature whining at the storm that doused the island. I peeked out of the front drapes to see lighting decorate the sky in striking random patterns. The thunder clapped like a drum and the rain bombarded everything. Alfred too sat, awakened from the storm, which gave him a reason to reach for his pipe and tobacco and to sit in what seemed like contentment. I laid on my back, hoping to fall into a peaceful sleep, but the crooked shadows that moved across the tent canvass only steeped my thoughts in fear.

The following morning, we were greeted with horrors. Next, to what looked like a ransacked campsite, half of the men that came with us to haul equipment vanished - no tattered clothing or blood that would suggest an attack could be found. The messy state of all the supplies could easily disguise hints of struggle, and due to the heavy rain, any traces of prints were washed away. I could not collect my thoughts quick enough before Wilbur came running over in a panic.

"Gael, he's gone. Silas is missing too. Him, the men . . . what the hell is going on?"

"I'm not too sure, let's not be too rational, maybe they went to seek better shelter in the peak of the night."

"Not likely" replied a voice in the distance.

Out of the tall grass nearby one of the tents, Silas appeared.

"There have been disappearances, likely because of the people who live 'ere."

"What'd they do? What do you mean?" I asked.

Silas looked at me, eyes wide with terror. He remained silent at the question and paced around before turning back to myself and now Alfred and Madina, who joined in on the conversation.

"We must go on, just a few miles forth and we'll have reached the dig site," said Silas as he checked his person ensuring he still had his tools around his waist.

"How can we ignore this!" said Alfred, shaken by the discovery.

"Because it is not our land! We're guests here! These are wicked people you hear. We have no say, they have no law, we can't even prove it was them! I've seen plenty o'er 'ere, and this isn't the worst. Get all o' your shit together, and we'll make way."

Alfred looked at me, and I could see his hand move towards the inside of the coat he wore. I could only presume he meant to reach for his pistol, but with Madina now moving toward Silas, he seized up.

The next few hours were met with silence. None would dispense a word to another, and I could only imagine what all of us who continued to the dig site were thinking of. *Where did the rest of us go? Were they killed? Where were the bodies? The tracks?* Disappearances in the middle of the storm didn't seem to keep us from discovery; there was a shroud of hope amongst us, even though we seemed to be surrounded by a sea of malign happenings.

After what felt like a lifetime had gone by, we had reached the fore-mentioned dig site. It was nothing like I would have imagined it to be. Other than the faint tale that my ears brought in of the young boy in the Kirihyyl mountains, discovering a place of gravestones, I hadn't much of an idea of what the site would look like. It was astonishing. Trees taller than any I had seen in my lifetime reached up to the grey sky above, cascading a barrage of darkness and shadow below, blocking out almost all the light from above. Gravestones littered the land for what could be a few kilometers; up and down rolling hills, near brooks and spreading up the mountains in the distance. Giant gothic monoliths stood high and decrepit. Everything was covered by bushes and trees and vines and dirt.

An eerie feel dawned on the mind and seemed to keep me on alert. A putrid smell lingered in the air like the smell of rotting bodies never buried, but who would come out here to bury their own so far from the shores, let alone not actually bury them?

Birds did not nest in these trees, but crows could be heard teasing us from a distance. Further away, I could see tents pitched and supplies everywhere; lanterns hung from crosses and stood on gravestones. A place where some tents stood, I could see piles of stone as if the workers tore down some of the graves to make room for their materials and sleeping quarters. A more massive tent was set up a distance away. I investigated to find that its canvas was shielding stone steps that led below the ground. It seemed that the workers had broken up essentially a large stone structure with a massive stone slab covering an opening. I inspected one of the pieces to see some markings etched into the stone, and had asked what the entire slab looked like before being broken, but the workers made no notes of it and took no pictures. All they said were that an intricate depiction of death was formed on the front and that the original four men who broke it open disappeared in one of the nights.

This made me shudder because no one seemed to care about the disappearances of all these men. No one tried to memorize their names, and no one attempted to question their vanishings except myself, in which I was met with murmurings under breath and swift movements of the hand implying I should leave it alone.

The graveyard was quite dense with the homes of the dead, but I did my best to not let the dark sensations take over my thoughts.

"Here it is," proclaimed Silas with almost a sense of joy.

This to me seemed odd, for what joy could be found while desecrating the graves of the dead and forgetting the souls of workers? The silence between the group carried on up until about what would've been night time – it was hard to tell because of the overgrowth of large trees which shielded the sun or moon above. Alfred approached myself and Madina as we sat on cots and drank tea brewed from leaflets I had brought with me. A small sense of comfort this brought us, for the tea was from my home which now seemed on the other side of the earth from here.

"It's time to go," said Alfred, adjusting a water satchel he had strapped around his chest. "Get your shit together, we go in five minutes."

A rush of excitement and fear fell over me after those words. I could not tell if Madina felt the same, I hoped she did, but for some reason, it felt like a mistake as well. The intense yearning for discovery began to settle in, and I immediately forgot about anything else except for the glory that would be bestowed upon us if we found anything of value underground.

4

After the quick demand by Alfred for us all to gather our things and begin the venture underground, I could not help but think about the young boy from so many years ago. Walking down the stone stairway with its smooth stones and decaying plants around, cobwebs hanging in the corners only partially whisked away by the workers, I walked next to Silas to inquire of the boys' whereabouts.

"Err, missing," he told me, attempting to silence the matter after I inquired a little more. "They say he left this land at middle age, some time ago after the incident with Father Murrin. Him secrets were no longer secret, so he vanished in fear the folks here would do somethin'."

The tunnel underground seemed to put him on edge, and he refused to answer more about the boy, but now a feeling of anxiety clouded my thoughts as the tunnel grew colder as we went on. Water dripped from the dirt ceiling above, and I could see the look of fear on Wilbur's face, fear that the soil would give way and crush us all. Madina reassured him that the tunnel's reinforcements would hold, but he took the information with a bit of contentment and uncertainty. Madina and Alfred both seemed beyond excited for discovery was within arm's reach.

Into the blackness, we all headed only a few steps behind or in front of the other, wishing for daylight and a warm fire that would keep us warm. The cold water and the more than occasional arachnid maintained a distaste amongst the party due to our position underground. The constant splish-splash of every step was bringing me closer to insanity until we saw it, a small opening with moonlight cascading from a small hole up above. Below it was the now infamous stone monolith carved with intricate depictions of death and life, fortunes and relics of a past world, just as the boy had disclosed to Arthur Murrin years ago, and Silas unto me not long ago.

A sense of awe fell over every one of us as we all slowly inspected the stone creation. Amazing carvings of what I could only discern to be human filled most of the one side of the monolith, accompanied by images of idols, suns, talismans, food and vague depictions of what could be cities.

Investigating the piece, Madina scribbled notes into her pocketbook and attempted to sketch whatever she could. Wilbur proceeded to examine the back to be forced into a state of bewilderment.

"Come see this," he said with a giddy but shaky voice, standing still like the monolith in front of us.

We moved to the other side of the monolith to see a large carving of a body. The large piece of stonework in front of us that stood eight feet tall had carved onto the back of it an anatomical depiction of a humanoid, which for sure did not look human to any of us. I had never seen anything like it. It had immensely long arms and an extruded jaw like a beast; its skull had an elongated cranium in the horizontal axis and hands with odd fingers. The head did not seem to depict a place for eyes, but the legs of this creature were the only thing human-like, two legs providing it the ability to walk upright.

"Extraordinary!" whispered Madina softly, loud enough for us to barely hear her.

"What do you think it is?" I asked.

"Only God would know," said Wilbur, performing the sign of the cross with his right hand.

"Or it is beyond God," said Alfred who was pacing around the hub, inspecting the great piece of stonework while analyzing every tunnel around. "This must be of importance, why else would it be here," he said suspiciously.

"Ay, I don't think there be much else to see no?" said Silas, intrigued by the great thing that stood towering over him.

As Silas took a step back, a hollow thud was heard. He looked down to his feet to see a patch of moss overturned by his moving around. I proceeded to him and knelt to inspect the disturbed greenery. I removed the moss to reveal a stone slab. It was about one meter in length and width with a large engraving of a circle with smaller circles inside and around it.

Everyone huddled around the stone and Alfred proceeded to knock on it with a medium sized rock that was nearby. The sound between the two pieces suggested that there was an empty space below. Looking around, Alfred found a larger stone and called me over to assist in lifting it. I had known what his plan was by the look on his face. I went to him, bent down and lifted the stone with him on a count of three. We raised the stone nearer to the slab, and once again on another count of three with the assistance of Wilbur, we lifted the stone high above our heads and dropped it directly onto the center of the slab. With a loud crash, the slab gave way under the weight and impact of the boulder, cracking and revealing a stone way leading downwards into a darker passageway.

"I'll be damned!" cried Silas, coughing at the dust that had flown up from the destruction of the slab.

"What do you think is down there?"

Peering into the hole, I looked carefully, but my vision was impeded by the darkness that lay within.

"We must find out!" proclaimed Madina, moving towards the stairway. As she walked towards the hole, she wrapped a piece of cloth around a piece of wood and opened a canteen which I could only presume had alcohol within it. She struck a match and created a torch. With the illumination of the flame, the light revealed something disturbing. Among the first few steps and continuing down, pools of blood could be seen on each step, with more blood smeared across the stones of the walls, dripping so smoothly as to sound like water in a large cave.

"Christ," said Wilbur with a trembling voice, sweating profusely and taking a step back. "I'm not going down there! What the fuck!"

We all stood and stared at the blood, thinking of what to do next. The sight made me feel sick, causing me to almost puke. I looked around to see Alfred relatively calm with everything, then looked left of him to see Silas' eyes wide in horror. Fear got the best of him at that moment, and it took some time to get him calm. After doing so, by the looks of all our faces, it had been decided that we venture further down.

Madina being the first down the hole, bearing the torch, stepped slowly down each step attempting to avoid the pools of blood but finding it merely impossible. Startled at our visit, rats scurried along, fleeing into cracks in the walls. More blood filled the stairwell. After a short trip downward, the stairs turned into a landing, and then into another flight of stairs proceeding further down. Blood could be seen everywhere, and small pieces of flesh lay sprawled and ravaged with clumps of blood-soaked hair in places. The smell was so profound that it required us all to cover our faces with rags. Then the unimaginable happened. As we continued down, the stairs ceased, and we reached what seemed like a cliff in a vast underground cavern. We were met with a horrific sprawl of dead bodies, bodies that had been there ravaged and eaten long ago, as well as the bodies of the men that went missing one of the first nights, identified barely by what was left.

The sight left us all gagging as the thick red liquid of life painted the walls and drenched the floor. I moved further towards what seemed like the end of the room to find a large mirror, maybe 20 feet high and 10 feet wide. The others joined at my side as well all stared at this magnificent thing. The glass was extremely weathered, stained with dirt, blood, and black spots. Its frame looked as if it were made of bronze and copper, and had beautiful little red jewels or stones embedded amongst its beautifully crafted frame.

The mirror was nothing short of fascinating. I ran my fingers along the frame, and just as I went to touch the glass, a faint murmur could be heard from behind us.

"What do you suppose that was," asked Wilbur, visibly shaken.

"I'm not sure," I replied, putting my hand on Wilbur's shoulder attempting to ease his state.

Suddenly, a hand fell onto my shoes, making

me jump in panic. Looking down, I could see a man, a man whose face I could barely recognize for its disfigured and mangled state. His body was merely a torso, legs thrashed and skinned, bones were broken and his face almost peeling. The man's eyes were taken out, blood streaming from cavities and gashes, slowly dripping from what was left of his jaw. It was Cpt. Hale. Through the gargling of blood and with his last breath, Hale said one thing that all of us could make out perfectly.

"Run," he said, exhaling and dropping his head to the floor.

At that moment, a loud groan engulfed the room, and a chilling wind from nowhere appeared and began to swirl. The ground started to shake, and now a laugh began to rise above the noise that struck fear into us all.

"Ha, ha, ha, ha, ha", it went menacingly. "Ha, ha, ha, ha . . ."

The laugh grew louder and more sinister. Madina turned around, and by her expression, I could see she was looking back towards the side of the room with the large mirror in terror. Wilbur, Alfred and I all turned around to see Silas, on his knees, facing the large mirror with hands outspread as if in praise, laughing maniacally. Two objects I could see were in his hands, two red stones, like the ones fashioned into the large mirror frame. As the wind blew and howled, the cold air now became hot, almost too hot for us to breath.

"Ha, ha, ha, ha . . . Ha, ha, ha, ha, ha, ha, ha . . . HA, HA, HA, HA, HAA!"

The glass on the mirror now began to change in color. Reflections ceased to appear, and a blackness began to swirl within it. Then the winds stopped for only just a moment, and a loud roar blasted outward from the center of the swirl. The roar pushed us all back off our feet, and upon getting up, Silas was no longer on the ground in praise. He had vanished, and the horrific vortex continued to turn and turn hypnotically.

"We need to leave this place, now," screamed Madina, attempting to get up after being pushed back but was frozen in place.

She struggled to move as the swirling tornado of blackness from within the mirror began to manifest what I could only describe as a claw or arm of some kind. It was a limb from a creature which I could not explain, something so horrid looking that secreted liquid and its shape suggested anatomically infeasible limbs. The arm grabbed Madina and pulled her into the mirror as she screamed in terror.

"Gael!", she called out as she vanished.

Immediately after, two more of these horrific arms reached out and grabbed Alfred and Wilbur. They screamed as they too were pulled into the blackness. Then, two more hands came out and attempted to grab me as well. I struck one with the knife that I brought with me. It peeled back in a way that suggested it had been harmed, but then with such speed, it grabbed onto my waist, catching my arms at my sides and pulling me towards the swirling vortex, unable to move or struggle or fight back. It was then, everything went black.

I awoke flat on my back looking up at a dark orange sky with deathly black clouds. A tremendous headache crept in, and dizziness fell over me as I made multiple attempts to sit up straight. As the pain in my head subsided, I noticed I was sitting in a field. It wasn't a typical field with green grass and bees and birds flying around in what seemed like organized randomness, but the field was more a hillside, relatively flat but with some sort of brownish-grey grass, mostly riddled with small stones. The hills seemed to graze endlessly. I called out the names of my friends but was met with a dull silence. In a state of panic and confusion, I managed to spot in the distance a faint glow of red.

The march forward toward the shining red light atop the weird grass and stones was lengthy. It dawned on me that I had barely been affected with what I had just seen in the caves. I began to even question if what I had seen was real. This place with its eerie orange sky and large black clouds seemed to make me want to forget everything, but

I convinced myself that what happened was real and that this was a reality which I could not understand though I resided consciously within it.

I walked endlessly until the red light became brighter and brighter. Trudging up a slightly steeper hill, I came up to a view that was so astonishing that I almost couldn't believe it *was* real. An enormous structure stood proudly in isolation under the apocalyptic sky. It looked like a gothic cathedral but sculpted by inhuman hands. It was made of red stones like rubies and stood windowless and circular in shape with what I could only interpret as steeples standing so high as if they touched the sky with one singular tower in the center that stood taller and prouder than the rest, piercing the black clouds above. The walk from the hilltop to the magnificent structure took what seemed like half a day's journey.

Finding my way through the small hills, I passed rivers of black water against black and red rocks and swiftly moved through the little tangles of grass and small yellow flowers that grew in random places. After an exhausting venture, I finally arrived at the base of the enormous structure. There was no door, but merely an opening at what I deemed to be the front of the structure, covered in a cluster of grass and the small flowers.

From up close the structure had a weird sense about it, but then again, the entire place from which I awakened in had an odd feeling about it. I proceeded through the large opening which became narrower the further I walked. Eventually, I reached a large stone engraved with letters and writings depicting many things: life, death, sacrifice. They made me shudder because the depictions didn't include anything of man, nor did they represent any other body. It was almost as if I understood it without having ever known anything like it in my past.

As I walked around inspecting the dim room looking for anything that could give some information as to where I was, a loud boom echoed and rumbled, shaking the walls and ground beneath my feet. I looked around to investigate its source and found only narrow pathways which I could barely walk through without feeling claustrophobic. I proceeded through admiring the fascinating stone walls as they glimmered and shone a beautiful red. The walls seemed to move like water, pulsing and swirling yet solid when touched. Whispers broke the silence that consumed my surroundings. I looked over my shoulder and around, discovering nothing. The whispers became louder.

I reached what looked like a place of worship, with a low altar in the center of the circular room with small stone objects that I believed could be seated on, spiraling around the center. Once more I could feel I understood pictures that were drawn about the room, interpreting the wickedness they portrayed, as well as a deep love but for something other than what I could deem to be justified. Time seemed to have no effect in this place I was in. Hunger did not befall me, normal bodily functions seemed to not affect me other than that of emotion and consciousness.

I walked around the room toward another opening. As I entered, more whispers could be heard, but these were much different from before. I recognized them to be Madina's and Alfred's voices, but Wilbur's wasn't to be found. I quickened my steps and followed the sounds as they came through the opening. Undergoing a slight ascent, the path that now led to what I could only consider to be a refuge among my colleagues was blurred by whispers and speech that did not belong to them. The whispers were haunting and caused pain; they disoriented me, causing my brain to almost pulsate. I put my hands to my temples to alleviate the pain, but that had no effect. The pain got so intense that I had couldn't keep my wits about me. I screamed in agony holding my head in my hands and dropping to my knees to find that the whispers had now stopped, and I found myself in a new place, as if I had teleported as soon as I lost concentration.

I was in a giant colosseum type of area. It was enormous, with giant stones that stood about 15 feet high that were organized in a circular fashion around what I could see to be a massive hole in the earth, so vast it was as if a mountain once stood in its empty and gaping void. The sky above was dim, and a red moon hung hauntingly low. Small yellow flowers grew at random among the stone formations.

Suddenly, a menacing sound filled the area with tremendous rage. I ducked down behind a pile of stones, peeking over to look around. From afar I could see figures emerging from the shadows of the red rock. They began to spill out in fearful numbers. I could not make out what they looked like, but I knew that they were not human. A buzz filled the air, and an almost static feel dispensed from the air around me. Then I could see Madina and Alfred being walked out, practically willingly going towards the edge of the enormous hole in the earth, or what I only deemed to still be earth. I stared intently, unable to move from my position in fear of being noticed by anything. I felt helpless. As my colleagues approached the giant void, the air became colder, and a mist began to form. Thick fog engulfed everything and the large stones that circled the void started to pulsate. A few moments of silence passed shortly after my sight was completely impaired by the fog. Then a scream: such a horrible scream. Something I had never heard in my entire life. All I could hear was the agony of one voice, and then another, as the life within them seeped out in noise so horrible it hurt my very soul.

The fog began to dissipate, and as it did, the whispers started once again. My body started to ache, and my head began to pound. The pain was now twice as bad as it was before. I dropped to the ground, losing my breath while holding my hands against my ears. My eyes would not shut, and they burned as the environment swirled around me. I could see phantoms materializing as I rolled around.

Hallucinations of people stared at me with black eyes and stood in disgust. All this I could feel while enduring tremendous pain. Then, everything ceased. The fog that had engulfed me moved and I found myself at the foot of the great void. Beside me stood a man whom I knew. Silas. I was confused. Lost. I stood up to face the man whom I had only met so long ago. My mind was in a whirl, and I could not understand what was happening. I looked at him and spoke the first thing that came to mind.

"What is this place?"

"The beginning."

"The beginning of what?"

Silas walked around me, gazing up at the red moon that hung prominently in the sky, casting a light that was almost absorbed by the red stone below.

"Dear oh dear. Man can do nothing but disappoint! Ha, ha, ha! The donation of the body has been helpful, but the soul is more important, don't you think? Ha! Don't worry, you will wake up, and you will die, and your soul will be used. Freedom comes through certain sleep, Gael. Through Nine Eyes of the Deep, we collect the remains of what was once our kin. Through Nine Eyes we see, we hear, we . . . *evolve!*"

I found myself frozen in place. I stood afraid as Silas approached me, staring into my eyes with eyes of blackness. As he approached, his form began to morph, and a blackness arose from the void behind him, almost binding together. Then a flash and it was over.

I awoke in the city streets back home, naked and shaking. My body was scarred, and my hair was mostly lost. I was picked up by workers and brought to a sanctuary, but that's not at all what it really was.

5

From the cold water that drips and spatters onto the cold, damp floor, to the whining and whimpering and endless murmurings of other crazed men, this place is now my home. The guards, who barely walk by, to the men in the cells beside me, I know that no matter what I say, I will not be freed from this ward.

It's a cold and wretched place filled with silences and screams that would forever taunt and confine me. I know my mind will soon be lost, so I write to whomever of what I know to be certainly true. For some unknown reason, I sit spared from a horrific death. I am told that Kirihyyl continues to draw people in as it develops its lands, but I know all who go there will be taken. Do not try to discover what is hidden. Things are meant to be hidden, and some questions are meant to never be answered.

As I finish all that I can recall, the poor soul beside me whose name I do not know, continues to ramble what he always rambles.

"Curse her and her kin. Shrouded by night and by dreams, freedom draws through undisturbed sleep."

As the moonlight slowly beams in through the window high above the cell floor, I find that I can only speak to myself to comfort my soul. I understand I'll endure many years in this place as my bones turn brittle. My blood will cease to flow, and my mind will be lost in a complexity of madness and indescribable visions. Madness is never kind and I fear enduring it, so to be free, a chance will be taken to see a tragic end at the tip of a broken shard of stone.

END

About the Author

Steven L. Grybko, born and raised in Hamilton Ontario, entered the writing world at the age of 22. Now at 24, he released his first book *The Disappearance of William Cross & Other Tales of Terror*. From his current home in Alberta he continues to write fiction, drawing from music, movies, books, and his own personal experiences.

Lightning Source UK Ltd.
Milton Keynes UK
UKHW020852110819
347757UK00005B/160/P

9 780368 979033